MW01275405

SMART CHOICES

Book One

SANDY JACOBSEN

Available as Ebook

ISBN 978-1-960903-78-5 (Paperback)

ISBN 978-1-960903-79-2 (Hardcover)

Publify Publishing

1412 W. Ave B

Lampasas, TX 76550

publifypublishing@gmail.com

Dedication

To my best buddy Bill who always believed in me and supported my crazy ideas. My friend Dixie who is the character Dotty in this novel also deserves credit. Dixie sadly passed away before this novel was written.

Acknowledgment

My best friend, Dixie, started me on the journey to write the *'CHOICES'* novels. She collaborated with me on the events portrayed in Part 1 of *SMART CHOICES*. This became a silly game Dixie and I played with a scammer. Dixie suggested I include the text and e-mail messages between myself and the scammer in one of my novels. It took me some time, but eventually Part 2 of this novel came to me. I must confess - Part 1 of this novel is a true story.

Knowing that you probably suspect I'm a bit crazy, and it may be true. Dixie has now passed but lives on as the character - Dotty. She is greatly missed and is very likely looking down laughing at my embellishments of her character.

About the Author

What happens when your dreams turn into reality? Sandy Jacobsen writes a mystery novel. She has always been drawn to mysteries, whether on film or the written word. She finds herself consumed by the stories her mind creates and has branched out to an unknown territory from writing corporate business letters to penning down intriguing, eloquent, and enigmatic mystery novels that are absolute page turners. This is a fun and exciting venture for her and she knows that once you discover her fast-paced books you'll find them hard to put down.

While she was working at corporate positions for firms, she composed business letters. After her corporate career, she owned and operated an equestrian center. The first book she published was a dressage instruction manual. The process of writing mystery novels is an interesting and educational experience for her.

Never Alone Again is the first of four mystery novels she has written. Be sure to look for Turn Around & Don't Blink, This Is Who I Am, and Who's Guilty Now.

Read Me a Story

When I was a child, I read lots of books to my sight impaired grandmother. This is one of my favorite memories. As an adult, I took a watercolor painting class. The instructor asked us to paint something from our childhood that inspired us. I painted myself reading a book to my grandmother.

My artistic talent was only fair, but my painting brought back this cherished memory for me.

The best part of writing novels is making up the lives of the characters. It's a world of my own imagination. The stories are also a way to live vicariously through my characters.

Writing is an opportunity to create a world the way you would like it to be. What fun to make up people, get them into various situations and then figure out how to solve their dilemmas.

People ask me – Where do the ideas for your stories come from? To be honest, I don't know. Sometimes it's a dream. Other times I'm in the shower, driving downthe road, or cleaning my horse's paddock.

I never know what's coming, I just have to hold on tight and go for the ride to see where my imagination takes me.

Preface

Technology today has reached unbelievable levels. Big brother is watching, tracking, and recording your every move through smart devices that are truly very smart. It's what choices you make with the information collected by the smart devices that's important. The world wide web is full of useful information and some misinformation.

Missy is a bored middle-aged lady who hasn't embraced technology. Not realizing it, she has carelessly become involved with some misinformation on the web. She hadn't given much thought about the corrupt people lurking behind the scenes on web sites, and they have found Missy.

Thinking a guy in a pop-up dating ad was cute she clicked on it. That click has led her to engage in a cat and mouse cyber game with her new online friend that has turned frightening.

Missy is about to find out if the choices she has made in this game were smart choices that could give her the life she dreams of or end her life. One little click of the mouse on your computer can start you on a path with some very difficult choices. Will they be smart choices?

PART ONE

Chapter 1

Missy's curious and adventurous spirit is leading her into a questionable situation. She tries to lead a normal quiet life, but somehow Missy tends to stray off the beaten path with her strong sense of right and wrong. She's a petite pixie-like person who has not matured into the mid-fifty lady she should be. Missy has an optimistic, glass half full, and enthusiastic personality. She always looks for the good in people, which in some cases is a downfall.

Life has become a bit boring with the pandemic, but Missy is still happy and looking forward to better times. Spending time with friends and her outdoor activities takes up her time on sunny days. The cloudy days are spent working on the novel she's writing. Since she's retired from an eight-to-five job, this is how every day evolves.

Missy had a sheltered and happy childhood, but becoming an adult led to a breakup from her six-year marriage. She thought a loving husband had been her future, but now life has taken an unexpected turn. She just had not figured out how to turn it around.

Living alone is now a way of life that she's adjusting to. She has moved to a new home, is rebuilding her life, and getting acquainted with her new friends. Her best friend, Dotty who relies on Missy, is thrilled to have her companionship.

Dotty is also good company, and fills the gap left by the ex-husband. Dotty is in her late seventies, lives alone with her two dogs, and is a night owl who keeps company with several glasses of wine every evening.

There is never a day that goes by for Dotty without a call or visit with Missy. Even if Missy has visited Dotty, this lonely lady starts every evening with an hour-long call discussing her day and the soap operas they watch. One thing that's for sure, no one can out talk that lady.

Dotty is a dear friend and keeps track of Missy's life that she lives through vicariously. She has taken an interest in Missy's latest endeavor, writing a best-seller novel, and is her biggest supporter.

Now that Missy has taken up writing novels, it's taking over her life and her computer. With the writing she has found a new interest in life, and it's waking her up to lots of possibilities. She has discovered new emotions relating to the characters in her novel. The characters are having great adventures making her restless and unsure of why she feels this way.

Missy likes her simple uncomplicated life living with her animals and the small group of friends she visits and talks to. Why would she want to interrupt her life and make a change? She has lived in big cities, worked at the hotel her parents owned, and now enjoys the ability to relax in a small town on her manageable income and quiet lifestyle.

There are still some things Missy is not willing to give up from her past. One of them is her 'dumb' phone, commonly known as a flip phone. She refuses to move into the smartphone era. All of her friends have them and she figures if she needs the information on one, she can have her friends look it upfor her.

Today Missy is at home working on her book when she hears the one thing that annoys her the most. Missy says to herself, "Crap, there it is again, that damn little beep from the cell."

She knows it's a text message. Over and over this is what bugs her. Missy wants to know why they can't talk to her. She would give an immediate response to whatever they wanted. She misses talking to people. With the crazy pandemic and social distancing, Missy feels terribly isolated.

Trying to ignore the phone, Missy continues thinking about reading a short crummy text message. Even worse, they expect her to text back. She's getting better at typing texts on her dumb phone, but it's a pain in the butt. Pushing the buttons once, twice, or three times for each letter.

Missy's thoughts are, 'Hello, my cell is on me 24/7. How hard is it to scroll to my name and push talk? I'd pick up right away. Are these people so busy they can't spare five minutes to talk to me? Why is it so much better to punch in a text that I might not decide to answer?'

Most days for Missy start with turning on the TV. The morning news she wants to watch doesn't come on. The discovery channel she has been watching a lot comes on. The damn smart TV is monitoring her program choices and turns on whatever channel 'IT' thinks she wants to watch.

The damn computer does the same thing. Ads pop up related to everything she searches for on the web. A lot of the subjects she searches are for research regarding her novel. She really doesn't want to buy an AK47 rifle and isn't interested in recovery for heroin addiction.

Chapter 2

———————————

Missy occasionally gets berated by Dotty for only using the basic technology. She thinks Missy should be more advanced because she's younger. Dotty too, who is twenty years older than Missy, has also ignored the latest technology, and uses her age as an excuse.

Missy checks in on Dotty each day to be sure her health is stable and to keep her company. Dotty tends to be a loner and has a bit of a depression problem, hence the wine consumption. She is pleased Missy calls and stays in touch but feels Missy should move on with her life and not be so stubborn.

Unknown to Dotty, Missy has moved on with her life and is now involved with a secret online friend she found on the internet. It was one of those pop-up ads that appear if the computer thinks you would be interested. It probably came up from something she researched for her novel.

She hadn't wanted to get involved with anyone, but the guy in the pop-up ad looked friendly and cute. Anyway, she could pretend to be someone else and therefore stay anonymous. It was sort of like creating a character in her novel and would be harmless.

Missy spent a few minutes thinking about her new friend and what she would say to him next. She had only been texting back and forth with him for a few days, but was a bit concerned about his kisses and hugs text. The messages were mostly impersonal and easy, so she didn't worry too much.

A text message came on her phone, but it wasn't from her new internet friend she would be pleased to hear from. Peeved, she read the text from her friend Pam. "What's up?"

She wants to type a text back, 'the sky asshole', but she decides to ignore it. Pam is always too judgmental, and Missy was not in a mood for that.

She was lost in her thoughts about text messages she would send to her online friend and realized she hadn't given Pam a return text. Frustrated with the text message and not wanting to make a text reply, Missy picked up her dumb phone and called Pam. "Hey, got your text. What's up with you?"

Annoyed, not wanting a long conversation, Pam answers, "I asked you first. You're so weird lately, I never know what you're up to."

Missy thought about what was just on her mind and wondered if she should tell Pam about her 'online friend'. "You wouldn't believe it if I told you."

Pam laughed, "Knowing you it could be anything. Why don't you surprise me."

7

Missy decided against telling her anything about the online friend. She can't think of how to bring up her new friend over the phone. The conversation would end with Pam chastising her for not asking her advice prior to connecting with this man. Pam can be such a know-it-all. Maybe it would be better to start with Dotty and get her reaction first.

Missy avoided the subject, "I'm just working like mad on my novel and trying to avoid people who might have the virus. It's a good thing I have the novel to work on since I'm spending so much time in the house. What are you doing to keep busy?"

"Same old stuff. Hey, got another call, have to go."

Missy is relieved in one way because she successfully avoided telling Pam about her online friend, but also annoyed at being brushed off by Pam's next call. Another tech advancement she dislikes.

After she hung up from talking with Pam, still thinking about her online friend, Missy called Dotty.

"Hi, I have something I want to run by you. I'll come over. It's something for show and tell."

Due to the nature of the conversations with her new online friend, Missy thinks it would be better to show Dotty the text messages from her phone. This is something that needs to be done face-to-face. The way people should talk.

She has typed the text messages on her computer and printed them. It's not something easily explained over the phone, and she wants Dotty to read everything that was said by this fellow and her.

Always eager to see Missy, Dotty is intrigued since she admittedly lives vicariously through Missy.

"Come on by, I just put on some coffee. Is this a new story you're writing or something else you've gotten yourself into?"

Missy knows the coffee invitation means Dotty is expecting an hour-long visit, which will probably be about right for their discussion of the online friend.

To please her friend, Missy will tell her about the venture into the online world of dating. Dotty will be blown away that she would choose this medium as way into the tech world.

Dotty has noticed and confronted Missy about a change in the way she has talked and acted lately. She probably thinks it has something to do with the novel Missy is writing and the crazy way the story is unfolding in her brain.

Missy had been satisfied without a man in her life, but after developing the characters in her novel, she is rethinking her decision and is interested in a new relationship. This online man might not be anything that would work out, but he seems safe enough. Besides, he sent her photos of himself in a uniform.

So far their communication has only been text messages which are not her choice, but that is all she is getting from her new friend. She hasn't been able to talk to him on the phone. His phone number only accepts text messages.

Chapter 3

Missy gathered her printed pages and drove to visit Dotty. She passed a car on the way down the road to Dotty's house. As Missy entered the house she asked, "Hi Dotty, who was that coming out of your driveway?"

"Clark, the computer man, I can't get the printer to work again."

Missy knew better, "I think you just like having him come over. That's a new printer. It should work perfectly."

Dotty looked insulted and defended herself, "Nonsense, why would I spend good money to pay him for nothing."

Missy continued with, "You're not that technology challenged, and I think you use any problems as an excuse to see Clark."

Dotty had to change Missy's accusation and thought of a solution, "You should have him over to your house for a bit of computer instruction. He's very nice looking and single. Maybe you should take a hint from the woman in your novel and think about finding a new man in your life."

Missy, thinking Dotty was clairvoyant, confessed, "Funny you should bring that up. Let's get our coffee. I have something to show you."

Realizing she should start with an explanation of how her online friend came to be, Missy asked, "Remember back a few years when you met that guy on a dating site? Did you have to pay for a membership?"

"You mean Gordon? I met him on one of them, but I don't know if I paid any money." Dotty's curiosity getting the best of her wondered, "Why do you ask?"

"I looked up one for research on my novel, but I didn't use it because you have to pay with a credit card. I don't trust using my credit cards on websites, so I didn't continue."

Getting to the point Missy added, "Anyway you know how companies send pop-up ads relating to stuff you look up online?"

Responding to Missy's question Dotty rattled on, "Yeah, that happens all the time. I get so mad, and I don't know how to stop it. I asked Clark about it, and he said to be wary of clicking on uncertain sites when searching for information. What else is the computer for but to look up stuff you want?" Dotty could rattle on forever if Missy let her. She is a sweet lady but did have a few quirks.

Missy had to interrupt her, "Well my computer did just that. An ad popped up a couple days ago and there was a photo of this nice-looking guy who wanted someone to chat with. The ad said to click on the photo. I did and then it said to send a text message to this number.

He had a nice smile and looked sweet, so after I clicked on his photo, I sent the text 'Hi' to the number with my phone. The next thing you know, I got a text message from this guy."

With the strangest expression on her face, Dotty said, "You have to be kidding. Why on earth would you do such a crazy thing? You have no idea who is sending the text message or if the photo is a real person. They could be tapping into all the information on your computer. It could be cyber stalking like they warn you about on TV."

Missy wanted Dotty to know she was careful, "I used a fake name and only a first name. I'm not going to reveal my location or any personal information. There isn't any vital information on my dumb phone. Look, I've typed out all the text messages between Rod and myself."

Suspicious, Dotty asked, "Messages, how long has this been going on?"

"For only about four days. He's a soldier in the army in Iraq. He sent me these photos of himself in his uniform. It's him because you can read his name on his uniform in this one. They match the one I originally clicked on. See these are the photos on my phone. He's nice looking isn't he."

Dotty took her time checking the photos and was not convinced. "He has nice teeth."

Missy was surprised, "Is that all you can say?"

Dotty started again, "Those photos could be anybody. Just because his name is on the uniform doesn't mean the guy who is texting

12

you is the same person. The guy texting you might not even be a soldier. What else do you know about this guy?"

Missy felt she had to defend herself, "Not much, there are only a few text messages back and forth. This is fun and I can't see any harm. Maybe this soldier is just lonely and wants someone to talk to. Why not text him back?

I went through my phone and typed everything on the computer, printed it, and I'm keeping a record. That way I can keep track of what he says and if there is anything suspicious in them. These are the messages I've printed out."

March 14

ME   Hi - Your photo popped up on my computer today with a message - 'Text this number to chat', so here I am. I live on a farm with a horse, goats, chickens and a dog. I've never done an online chat but thought it would be fun. Julie

ROD   Thanks Julie am going to enjoy communicating with you. It's really boring here at times and I want to talk with someone back home.

ME   Where are you now?

ROD   I'm here in Iraq, am here on mission I was deployed December after the killing of Iranian terrorist.

ME   Where do yo live in the US?

ROD   Dallas, TX I live with my daughter. No parents, I was an orphan.

ME   How long will you be in Iraq?

ROD   I will be leaving in not less than two months am retiring completely.

ME   What are your hobbies?

ROD   My hobbies here are music, dance, traveling, my family, football, swimming, beach walk with my partner, movies, intellectual discussion as well as sitting in front of the fireplace. How about you?

ME   I like hiking, golf, cycling and playing with my animals.

ROD   You are free to ask me anything you want to know about me OK.

ME   Okay let's play 20?'s What is your favorite ice cream flavor?

ROD   Chocolate and strawberry.

ME   What is your favorite type of food?

ROD   Chinese food - hope is what you meant?

ME   What type of vehicle do you drive?

ROD   You mean when I arrive in the state? Pick up

ME   I have a pick up too.

ROD   Really that means we have something in common.

ME   Do you prefer beer or wine?

ROD   I'm not the drinking type, but I prefer wine.

ME   Sorry for the delay. I'm hiking now and it's hard to text. I'm not very good at it.

Next day

ROD   Good morning.

ME   Sorry I just now saw your text.

ROD   Okay what time do you have there?

ME   7 AM, I just got up.

ROD   Okay babe that's nice have you had your coffee already?

ME   Yes, am feeding the dog.

ROD   Ok what do you think about me?

ME   Not sure, since we only text.

ROD   I'll send you a photo from here.

ME Okay, It's hard to say much on text, email would be better. Do you have one? We could also write letters. I'm - juliebuddy2@gmail.com

ROD   It's easier for me to text. I'm so sorry for that you have to understand that nature of my job. As it stands now I need a help but don't to go about it.

ME   Things are difficult here too with the virus.

ROD   It's really hurts that this virus is taking a very big impact in the world. How I wish this would just disappear.

ME   Me too.

ROD   Yes, I pray it goes off as soon as possible.

ME   Have you had an online relationship?

ROD   My perception of an ideal relationship: To me one who truly care about the things that God has created for us, like the trees, the flowers, and nature. A wise man once said, "If you don't reach out your hand, no one will take it. "Are you willing to take my hand, walk through life with me, and share our live together.

ME   That is serious.

ROD   Do I look like Im here for games or joke?

ME   No, sorry.

ROD   I'll send photos so you can see me

Day 3

ROD   Hi sweetie how are you doing over there? Am sorry I couldn't write you back on time I was on active duty as the Taliban terrorist attached the camp yesterday I guess you are sleeping now write me when you are awake take care sleep tight kiss and hugs.

ME   Going for another hike with my dog today. Not much else.

ROD   I want you to know that you are always in my heart and I think about you here always I love you yesterday today and tomorrow and forever.

Day 4

ROD   Would you like to meet?

ME   Yes, sure

ROD   Do you live alone?

ME   No, with a roommate.

ROD   What kind of car do you have?

ME   SUV

ROD   How many times do you work in a week.

ME   Not working, retired

ROD   Okay what was the nature of you job before you stopped"

ME   Office jobs

ROD   Okay

###

Dotty looked up from the pages with a frown on her face and shook her head.

"You can't tell from all that crap who this guy is after only four days. And, what's with the love stuff? Is that all you have?"

"That's all I have so far," was all Missy could say. Dotty's comments did leave Missy slightly concerned.

Dotty was ready to give Missy a mouth full, "I knew there was something going on with you besides the crazy way you're writing that novel. You come up with some strange ideas, but this one is way over the top. You have no idea who this guy is and what he's up to. Can't you think of something more productive to do with your time. What about your novel? Why isn't that enough to keep you busy."

Missy justified her new preoccupation, "Dotty, you've been pestering me to move into the twenty-first century. Well, now I'm doing that. Online dating is the newest thing.

It's not like I'm dating him anyway. We're just texting back and forth. I even made up a new email address to use instead of my main one. I think this is safe to do. Besides, he's in Iraq and I'm not going to tell him where I'm living."

Dotty wasn't going to give up, "Missy don't be so naive, those two photos don't show where he really is. He could be fake and anywhere in the world. What about the number he texts from?"

"I can probably find that out, but for now I just want to see where this goes."

Missy was getting tired of this interrogation and made up an excuse to leave, "Look, I need to get to the store. Don't be such a worry wart. I'll keep you posted."

Chapter 4

Leaving Dotty's house Missy started to think about the recriminations regarding her new online friend. Maybe Dotty had a point. The only attraction she really had to this guy was his handsome smiling face. One thing that did bother her was the poor spelling and sentence structure of his text messages. Granted, a lot of people abbreviate words and construct short sentences when sending text messages, but this didn't always make sense.

Even more bothersome was the last couple text messages expressing his love and the kiss and hug stuff. He didn't even know what she looked like or anything about her. Why would he write that sort of thing? He looked perfectly normal in the photo, but there was something off about this guy.

For now, she would continue to respond to his text messages and see what happened. He said his retirement was soon. Maybe he would come back to the states, and she would see him. Another thing that puzzled her, was the inability to talk on the phone. Obviously, he had a phone because he sent texts. It was also confusing that his phone only accepted text messages. Why doesn't he have a normal phone? With a normal phone, he should be able to call because her phone number probably showed up on his phone.

All these questions were beginning to make her doubt whether she should continue with him. On the other hand, what if this guy is just a lonely soldier who wants someone to communicate with? As long as she was careful what could be the harm. Besides, she was bored and at least it was something new.

The next morning Missy went to the kitchen for coffee and the little green light indicating a text message was flashing on her phone. A bit of excitement filled her as she picked up the phone and scrolled to messages. She wondered why she would be excited, and should she be?

Sure enough it was a text message from Rod. Missy responded to the text message even though her phone indicated it came at 3:47 AM. She realized there was a time difference between Iraq and the US, so she didn't think too much about it.

Within minutes Rod responded and she continued the text conversation in her limited capacity for texting. If only they could communicate like normal people talking to each other. Texting back and forth was such a pain.

###

ROD   Hi dear how are your doing today.

ME   I'm fine, how are you?

ROD   Okay that good but bit bored here I wish I can get something to keep my busy and company here. Do you go out for shopping?

ME   Yes, for groceries.

ROD   I thought stores are shot down? I really need a favor from you don't know if you can help me with it. I need a favor so I can be able to play games

online here. Go to a store or Walmart to get me a Google Play card or an iTune card hope you are not thinking negative or otherwise.

ME   I don't know what an iTune card is. How do you use it?

ROD   All you do is to buy it from the stores scratch it send me the numbers to redeem it here. Ask for an iTunes card in the store can you get one for me today?

ME   I'll try.

ROD   Okay thanks I really appreciate   Are you still going for hiking today?

ME   Yes

ROD   Okay good keep doing what makes you happy

As soon as Missy determined the text messages had ended, she typed out both Rod's and her texts.   She reread what had been sent between them and started to reevaluate Rod.   Not being very techy, Missy didn't have any idea what an iTune card was.   She didn't have a smart phone that used apps for iTunes, and her dumb phone didn't have that capability.   She had never played any games or music on her computer either.

Why would he want her to buy him an iTune card and need one to play games? What games? Missy had seen her friends play games on their smartphones. She knew there were apps to load games and other stuff on a smartphone. Was this what he needed? Why didn't he have access to other technology to play music or games?

The one thing that also bothered Missy was his inability to get the card himself and why would he need one? Surely the army had every type of technology available to soldiers. She wanted answers. This online friendship had just taken a turn and she didn't like where it was going.

She needed to go to the grocery store today anyway, so she would ask a clerk about the location of the iTune card in the store and also see how much a card cost.

Missy approached a clerk in the entertainment department, "Hi, can you show me where the iTune cards are?"

"Sure, over here. Are you buying this for yourself?"

Thinking that was a strange question Missy answered, "No, for a friend."

The clerk looked at Missy with a suspicious face, "We have to ask because these cards are used by scammers so often."

Missy was suddenly shocked to think Rod was probably a scammer. Feeling silly and naive, she lied to the clerk, "I'm sure my friend is okay. I've known her forever."

Missy also noticed the lowest price for the card was twenty-five dollars. She wouldn't want to spend that much money for a stranger she didn't know anyway. Those little doubts that had been in the back of Missy's mind were now out in front as she walked out of the store. The minute she would get home, she was going to Google iTune scammers and educate herself.

Missy's emotions ran from stupidity to anger. Somehow she had become involved with a scammer from that website she clicked on. The soldier in the photos was very likely having his identity used to lure her in. Who knows what type of person has been texting her.

Thank God she didn't give out any other information than her cell number.

She also felt violated by this guy. The question now was what to do about it. Besides herself, this soldier was a victim. More than likely the soldier had no idea his identity was being used. This bothered Missy even more than what this scammer guy was doing to her.

The soldier was in the military risking his life to defend her country and this scammer guy was using him to steal money. Who was this scammer guy and where was he? Dotty had asked her about the phone number the guy was using. Missy tried to call the number, but a recording came on again saying it was for text messages only.

Next she Googled the number. It was from a company named Broadband in Carrollton, Texas. Interesting, since this scammer guy said he lived in Dallas and Carrollton is very close to Dallas according to the Google map Missy pulled up. As much as she hated technology, it had come in handy.

There was no doubt in Missy's mind this guy was a scammer. Her real concern wasn't for herself, she could easily end this relationship, but what about the soldier. How would he know this was happening to his identity? Somehow she would try to inform him about the scam.

It was very likely this guy was also scamming dozens of other women. Missy Googled 'US Army scams' and found a site to use as a platform to notify the army of a potential scam. Missy pulled a form up, filled it out with all the information she had gathered, and sent it off.

Wow!, The next day a lengthy email came back that warned her to cease communication with this scammer. There was also a page and a half with more information about scammers. This was not an education she would ever consider, but now knew more than she wanted.

Unfortunately, she also found out the army would not reveal any information about a soldier. They wouldn't even verify there was a soldier named Stoddard in the army. Could that photo be fake too? No, this had to be a real person in the photo. He was in uniform standing in front of an American flag in what looked like a recruiting office.

Missy was disappointed she couldn't notify the soldier, but maybe she could do something about the scammer guy. She would have to give this a lot of thought and it would involve research. This was not how she would like to spend her time, but she couldn't let it go. As much as she hated the scammer, the thoughts of the soldier stayed with her.

Chapter 5

The next day several text messages came from Rod. Missy wasn't sure how to respond, so she ignored them while deciding what to do. After quite a bit of thinking for a couple days, she decided to turn the tables on the scammer guy. Missy was going to beat him at his own game and string him along. One thing was for sure, she would never send him an iTune card. She replied to his text and since she was so inept at texting suggested emails and typed her fake email address in.

ROD   Are you home now? How did it go hope all is well with you over there?Sorry I couldn't write you back on time. I was asking if your are home from hiking? How are you?   How was your day? Why are your silent?

ME   Had trouble with my phone.

ROD   I thought as much cuz I have been sending you messages you are not replying unlike before Have you get it fixed now? Where are you at the moment? and what are your plans for the day?

ME   Hiking with my dog.

ROD   Okay good are you still going to city today as you said yesterday and what we discussed previously about helping me with the card?

ME   Not sure if I'm going to town.

ROD   Okay dear I'm waiting.   I will send you a photo so you see how it looks like OK

###

This appeared to be a determined scammer guy who was pressing Missy to get the iTune card and give him the numbers on the back. How would Missy reply to avoid sending Rod the numbers from the iTune card which she had no intention of buying. She had to come up with an excuse for the delay in responding to his previous text messages, but what should she say to string him along.   This was getting very complicated. She spent the entire day trying to figure out a strategy to outsmart this guy.

When she opened her computer the next morning, the answer was right in her emails. This was the first email from Rod, and it was a whopper.

ROD   One thing I would like to seek from you is HONEST I want us to be honest to each other in everything we do, of course you would agree with me that honest is the keep to a good and lasting relationship, without truth we cannot move forward. I believe in cooperate existence in my relationship which I believe is the best for a matured relationship.

One that will share my sorrows with me and one that will be there for me in terms of good and problems. You see, there are also a degree sequential. I may choose first TRUST and COMMUNICATION. They go hand in hand and without them any type of relationship, business, personal, family, whatever, is bound to fail. I will try to be more specific, I know what we just met which I agree that it is very unacceptable to earn someone's trust that you met in this form but at the same time it does not mean that there are not good ones who are honest and willing to give their being to ensure and I want you to know I need a woman who understand that my word is my bond is whom I seek, knowing that for while I am not even close to perfect, God is working in me. She is a woman who is family oriented, open minded, loyal, optimistic and God fearing. She should never be the last one to know my wants, needs and trouble, but the first one to know. We should complement each other so that later we will complete each other. Our relationship will be grounded in faith in the Lord and filled with mutual respect. A woman who is a firm supporter of the saying life is too short for drama and petty things, so kiss slowly, laugh insanely, love truly and forgive quickly Yes only you have a positive mindset not think negative cuz at time we are the ones who brought problem to ourselves cuz of negative thoughts I am open-hearted and optimistic. I enjoy every day of my life no matter how difficult life can be I am honest intelligent and confident person with a good sense of humor and friendly and kind I always respect people around me and I never judge but always try to understand I believe in real love I'm look for only serious relationship and I wish to live happily ever after I am active and full of energy. I have always goals and dreams which I try to make true can it be you?

It took Missy three times to read this email and process her decision to not continue with this guy who definitely wasn't an American Army soldier. He was probably one of several scammers sitting in cubes sending out text messages by the thousands. His spelling and grammar was terrible, besides the fact that his text messages were crazy.

Maybe this was dangerous, and she was already in over her head with this idea. Dotty was right and she should have listened to her. Missy needed to find a way to end this ridiculous game. Just then another text message came from Rod.

ROD   Did you get what I sent to you? I hope to hear from you positively thank and take care.

ME   I'm hiking with my dog.

ROD   Okay good, how long are you spending out there?

ME   About an hour

ROD   Ok be safe When are you gong to help me with the card is really important to me so I can keep myself company here

###

Now Missy knew for sure she had made a huge mistake clicking on the popup photo. Why did she think it was a good idea to play along with a scammer? She couldn't possibly be that bored, but obviously was that stupid. She needed to get back to reality. So far, she had made poor choices and needed to make some smart ones. The one person who seems to have a level head was Dotty. It was time to pay another visit to Dotty who would set her straight.

Chapter 6

Since Dotty was the only person who knew about Rod, Missy decided to show her the latest text messages and email. Dotty would be pleased she was going to end the scam, as Dotty thought it was a bad idea in the first place. Missy gathered the copied pages and headed to Dotty's house.

Missy called Dotty to let her know she was about to arrive with more from her online friend. Before handing the pages to Dotty, Missy acknowledged,

"Okay, read this and then you can say, 'I told you so'. I've decided enough is enough and I'll end this scam. I've come up with an email I'll send to Rod that will put an end to the scam. Here's the latest weird stuff he sent in an email."

Time dragged on as Missy impatiently waited for Dotty to read the pages given her. Like Missy, she had to reread the extensive email to understand what Rod had written. The look on Dotty's face when she finally finished said just what Missy expected, but of course she had lots more to say.

"What a bunch of crap. I can't believe he wrote all that crazy stuff. This is exactly what I've been afraid of. Every day I see something on TV about scams, especially those targeting the elderly. Maybe some of those dating sites are legit, but this one was a scam site. Didn't you say it was one of those popups?"

"Yeah, I think it came up because I was looking for information on dating sites for my novel research. I clicked on a couple that I found on Google," explained Missy. "Then a few days later, Rod's photo was in a popup ad. He was so cute, I couldn't resist."

This explanation from Missy didn't slow Dotty down, "The scammer, whoever he is, or it could even be a she, doesn't know how old you are or anything about you. They just want money or something from whoever clicks on their site. I guess they're looking for lonely or bored people who can be easily fooled. I'm sure you don't fall into that category, but I know you well enough that you can't let things go."

Dotty's last words led Missy to confess the rest of her work on the scam.

"This scam really has bugged me. It's the first time I've come across someone trying to scam me. So, I've done everything I could to locate the scammer guy. You suggested I check the phone number, so I did. I tried calling the number, he's using, and I got a message that it's for text only.

I Googled the number, and it came from a company in Carrollton, Texas. I even contacted the phone company but couldn't get anywhere. Mostly I feel bad for the real soldier in the photo. He probably doesn't know his identity is being used by scammers trying to cheat people out of their money.

I found an army web site to report scammers using army soldier's identities. I filled out a form and sent it. The army replied with an extensive email about criminals using soldiers' identities to scam people. Unfortunately, they won't divulge any information regarding soldiers, so it's not likely I will be able to let this soldier know what's going on. I don't care about the scammer, just the soldier."

Dotty wasn't finished chastising Missy, "I can't believe you've gone this far. If you're going to end the scam, why go to the trouble of trying to find the scammer and the soldier?"

Missy stood her ground, "I don't like the idea of someone trying to cheat or steal from me. These scam people ought to be in jail and those soldiers are risking their lives to protect us. Soldiers serving our country shouldn't be violated or taken advantage in this way."

Wanting to convince Missy she must end the game, Dotty added, "Missy, there are probably a million scams going on every day. Those people who scam are in some third world country and are among dozens working for some outfit making millions and paying the scam workers peanuts."

Missy was surprised Dotty would know this much about scammers and asked, "How do you know all this?"

"I saw a program on TV. It was one of those true crime shows I watch. It caught my attention after you showed me those first text messages from your 'online friend'."

Missy thought it best to relieve Dotty from worry, "As soon as I get home I'm going to send him this email that will end everything. Read this and you'll be satisfied. I'm going to be rid of the scammer."

When Missy got home she sent the email she had just shown to Dotty.

ME   I wish you were the soldier "Stoddard" in the photo. I would like him. You were busted with the iTune scam. I know all military personnel have an email account and can receive written letters. Shame on you for using the identity of a soldier serving my country.

Surprisingly Rod emailed right back.

ROD   Really if that's the way you conclude it no problem but I will love you make a more research about me, well thanks for your time and care I really appreciate I know from the onset you are always negative and have a doubting spirit bye I can never beg for love and attention when I meet the right woman I will know.

ME   A real soldier would not need an iTune card. Only a scammer who wants to cash it in.

ROD Cuz I asked you for an iTunes card you called me a scammer.

###

Missy hoped this would be the last text message and email from Rod. It did bother her that he professed his love for her again in an email. That was the one thing that had always seemed the strangest about him. Nobody falls in love with a person after no more than ten days of emails and text messages. Hopefully, he would move on to the next woman who was dumb enough to click

Too bad, because she still liked the soldier in the photo. He had such a kind face and looked like a nice man. She could certainly go for a guy who looked like that. Bummer he wasn't real. Once again she opened her phone, scrolled to message and looked at the photo of the soldier. Somehow she couldn't bring herself to delete it. Thankfully, the next several days were quiet, and she was relieved to have ended this mistake that she would never make again.

Missy was glad she confided in Dotty, her investigation into the scammer guy, and concern for the soldier. She was surprised at the minimal, 'I told you so', Dotty gave her. She deserved a lot more. Why hadn't she seen through the scammer as easily as Dotty? Maybe she was too naive and trustworthy.

There was a certain amount of trepidation in sending them, 'I know you are a scammer', email. On one hand, she was attracted to the soldier in the photo. She had been pleasantly anxious when a text message or email came from Rod when she originally thought he was the soldier. On the other hand, she was furious at herself for falling for the scam in the beginning. Regardless of how she felt, it was now over for good.

Chapter 7

———————————

F our days later, Missy's fears were realized when she opened her emails on the computer. He was back.

###

ROD Hi dear how are you? Is quite unfortunate you are using a negative thoughts to lose the good that is coming your way cuz I asked you for iTunes card you stopped talking to me and call me fake, I like you naturally am interested in you reply me back let's sort this out amicably thanks.

ME The clerk at the store told me the iTune cards are used by scammers.

ROD Really now you are judging and concluding from just what a clerk told you it's very much unfair things are not done that way. If I'm here for games I wouldn't have write you again but you should have tell the clerk that you know me and you just wanted to help she is just telling you for to be careful but all you do was think I can get it in Iraq I would have tell you to get one for me No but is only sold in the state Well that's bygone how are you? How is the virus cases over there? Hope you are protecting yourself and staying away from infected victims. Do you want to email me? You are free to write whatever you want to Secondly you need to know this I know there are bad people trying to impersonate that does mean everybody is bad or have evil intentions I only ask for help I never imposed it on you I explained the reason why I needed this card you said OK you gonna help. Coming back all I could get from you is calling me names, my dear is unfair you don't know what we are passing through here it's only the strong survives and the grace of God.

This email was a shock. Not only didn't Rod go away, but he was also laying a huge guilt trip on her. There was also the subtle way he was still asking for the iTune card. Maybe laying guilt trips on the scam victims was their way of worming themselves back after being rejected. What was it going to take to be rid of him?

Missy had to sit down and give her next response some serious thought. She needed time to think of something that would end this terrible mistake, so she would sleep on it. There was still the mix of anger and fear regarding this situation. This was getting to the point of scaring her.

Dotty was right. She was in over her head with this scammer guy, but it was difficult to let go. She had made an attempt to identify this guy, but maybe she didn't go far enough. If she couldn't get rid of him, maybe she could still find out where he was or any other information about him even though she knew it was a bad idea. What she needed was more information which would require extended research and additional time.

Procrastination was not working in her favor because the next morning there was a text message on her phone.

ROD   Hope you are fine wish you a nice and blissful day kiss kiss kiss   Okay I believe you have nothing to worry or doubt about me any more?   What time do you have there now?

ME   It's early

ROD   But I'm very bored here I still need what I asked from you previously hope don't mind?   I sent you an email now have you read it?

ME   No my computer isn't on.

ROD   Okay you do that later, can you be able to help me with the card today? Okay when possible can this be available? Hope you know what to tell to the clerk this time?

Missy was at a loss for what to text back. This guy was incredibly determined to get an iTune card. For now, she would just answer as short and simple as possible until she had a plan worked out. One thing was for sure, she wouldn't get him the iTune card he was still asking for. She needed to get him off the iTune subject if she was to move on to something that would get him to reveal himself.

Missy finished her brief text message and turned on the TV. The morning news came on. The story was all about the virus and how many people were losing their jobs. So many people were in jeopardy of not being able to pay rent or their mortgages, let alone pay for food.

That was just what she needed to hear. The economic effects of the virus would be her ticket to move away from the iTune card. Missy sat down at her computer and drafted an email for Rod. This was going to be her excuse for not getting him the iTune card.

She started to laugh as she typed. This was starting to be fun. The anticipation of his response was fueling her fingers as she typed.

What would he come up with next as a reason for her to get the card, and would he continue with the guilt trips and profess his love?

The email should be short and to the point. When she finished and was satisfied with the content, Missy clicked on send. Now that she was communicating with emails, it was also easy to forward them to Dotty. The emails were handy since all she had to do was print them from her sent file.

Missy added this one to the stack of emails and text message she was saving as a record of this crazy game she and Dotty were playing.

ME   Hi - I have thought about the iTune card and with the problems my neighbors are having losing their jobs, I feel I need to use any extra money I have to help them. I can't justify spending $50 on a card for your entertainment instead of food for my neighbors.

ROD   Hi Julie I got your last mail now what are you concluding on are you helping me with the card or not?

ME   I'm sorry but I feel spending money to buy food for my neighbors is more important than an iTune card for you.

ROD OK I see you do not feel for me here either or you are acting on what the clerk told you previously

ME   I do feel for you deeply but my moral compass is for my neighbors

ROD   Now I see you spending $50 to get me what will make me happy and put a smile on my face here is now a much thing to you no problem God is watching everyone Thanks

ME   This has nothing to do with the clerk I just have my priorities sorry please understand. I also contacted the US Army and they sent me a long letter warning me about scammers using soldiers identity and wanting iTune cards.

ROD   I Okay I see you have decided in what to do... Why the sudden change of mind you promised to help me with one, had it been the clerk did not tell you bullshit the day you went to the store you would have helped me for long but I see you are acting according to what the clerk told you previously no problem things are not done that way in life goes on. Okay you really have made up your mind not to help me thanks

ME   I hope we can still remain friends

ROD   Why do yo ask such a question?

ME   Because I value your friendship and don't want to lose you

ROD   Really how sure I'm I with this you just said now? Well I'm having problems with you. just that you fail to understand me but no problem we are friends and lovers cuz I care about you and think about you here always

ME   Me too I'm going out for my hike now

ROD   Okay write me when you are back take care by for now

Missy was finding communicating that quickly from her email directly into his email was difficult. She was having to think too quickly. She almost blew it with the stuff about contacting the army. But maybe that was a good thing. It would let him know she was not totally sold on him and was still skeptical. It was fun making him confused about her loyalty.

A thought came to her. Where along this crazy venture did she decide to continue with the scam? Wasn't she scared a couple days ago? Now she was racking her brain to think of more ways to get back at him. Where had this venture taken another turn? Was it his determination that fueled hers? Oh well, she was used to writing and this was just the same thing. Yeah, sure.

She was going to make him work for the scam. This was not going to be easy for him. She could come up with the same crazy stuff he did. She would string him along and see where this bizarre plan would take her. Time to come up with some stuff to keep his interest and try to get more information about where he was from him.

Missy got out her tablet, sat down at her desk, and started developing a storyline for an email to Rod. After all, she was a writer and seemed to be able to come up with lots of great ideas for her novel. This was just the same use of her imagination. She would be careful to not give too much information about herself that would reveal her identity or whereabouts.

Chapter 8

———————————

The next morning after coffee and breakfast Missy sat down at her computer. After reading the morning paper and going through Facebook, she opened her email. There wasn't anything from Rod. She opened her tablet, typed an email from the latest drafts she had created for Rod, and clicked on send.

###

ME   Hi - I'm a single lady and have never had an online relationship before, so am a bit Leery. I like your photo and you seem like a nice guy, but you are a long way from here. I spend my days playing with my animals and talking to my friends since people are not supposed to gather due to the virus. I like a lot of sports - golf and tennis. I live between the mountains and the ocean, so I can hike a lot.

ROD Hi Julie how are you? I got your message thanks for telling me more about yourself wish you a nice and peaceful day ahead Yes thank for your wonderful hand of friendship but I need to see more of your pictures I miss looking at it. Remember you are the only one I have you are my family I must confess I have found love and happiness in you I can't afford to lose you promise me you will always stand by me no matter any circumstances

ME I'll take some photos and send them.

ROD OK good thanks am waiting OK good hope all is well with you? How you eaten? OK take care of yourself over there do have it in mind that someone like things are always love you kiss kiss

Rod's last emails were a relief from asking for the iTune card, but he was still professing his love and that bugged her. The give-away that he was probably in a third world country was his lack of the correct English language.

Missy's anxiety and fear of the scammer was beginning to diminish as she now was sure he would never find her, and she wouldn't be in danger.

She also decided a few photos of herself would be harmless, so she made a couple and sent them. Her plan to string the scammer guy along was working. Maybe if she kept him busy, he wouldn't have as much time to scam someone else.

ME   (text with photos) Sent two photos

ROD   (text) Wow beautiful

ME   (text) Yeah, thanks

To be fair to Dotty, Missy went to her house to confess the plan to continue with the scammer.

Dotty exploded with, "I thought you were going to end this crazy game. Are you out of your mind?"

"Dotty just read the last stuff I wrote after I changed my plan to identify this guy. It's obvious I can't get rid of him, so I'm going to mess with him hoping he will slip up and reveal himself. "

Dotty read the emails from Rod and Missy. As she continued, Missy saw a smile start on Dotty's face and soon she laughed too.

"This guy is nuts, and you're right, he has to be from a third world country the messed-up way he writes. I guess you're safe enough as long as you don't give out too much information about yourself and your location.

The idea of photos may not have been the wisest though. I'm also curious to see what he comes up with next. I know I've been after you to end this silly game, but I have to admit it is kind of fun. Maybe we can get on one of those talk shows and tell everyone what a couple of bored dummies we are."

Dotty's opinion gave Missy the encouragement and incentive to keep the ruse going.

"I'll keep typing and printing the emails and text messages, so we have a record. Someday we'll sit back, read these, and have a huge laugh."

Missy was thinking how clever she was until several days went by without a text message or email from Rod. Maybe he had moved on to another lonely old lady, or there was something about her photos that turned him off. It could be he wasn't convinced she was really interested.

His text message that finally came a few days later confirmed her last thought was the correct one. She would need just the right response to fix this problem. Since he was expressing so much love, she might need to somewhat match his desires. Of course, she wasn't going to go overboard the way he did. Just express her concern for his safety which would be logical and wanting to continue to be his friend.

###

ROD   Hi Julie how are you? Sorry I couldn't write you on time. I just came back from patrol. I hope all is well with you? You did not bother to check on me why?

ME   You're right, sorry, I'm not sure you can discuss what you do over there and am maybe afraid something bad will happen to you.   I want to think you are always OK so I don't ask, please forgive me. I am still trying to help my neighbors.

Over the next several days, Missy only got text messages from Rod. Once again he was asking for the iTune card. The ploy of spending her extra money to buy food for her neighbors was not working. Missy waited to see if he got tired of the response about feeding neighbors instead of buying him the card. If buying food for the neighbors wasn't a good cause, what would be?

She was beginning to wonder if he even read her text and email responses. If he did read them, it didn't make any difference because he stayed on the same course. If he didn't get the card, would he come up with something else to ask for? The next responses from Rod didn't have anything to do with the card or her neighbors.

###

ROD   Hi Julie How are you? Hope all is well with you over there

ME   Hi I'm fine, just worried about my neighbors and this ever growing virus.

ROD   Hi dear how are you Sorry I have not been able to reply to your email I have been very busy here I will do that as soon I free OK

When nothing new came from Rod, she decided to add some pressure. Why not ask him to pay for his own card? She was betting no one had ever asked the scammer for money. That should get a very informative response. Missy was sure soldiers were paid and would very likely send money home to wives or other relatives.   Rod's response was the exact lie she anticipated.   How dumb do these scammers think their victims are?

ROD   Here is night but not on patrol tonight Julie I really need what I have been asking from you here can you grant me my request for me to be happy and keep myself company here

ME   I will try, but I have to wait till May 1st when I will see how much my neighbors need and how my bank balance is. Can you send me the money?

ROD   Oh Julie this is just April 3rd you are telling me to hold on May 1st is not fair you have to put yourself in my shoes please be considerate for once well you still don't want to understand me soldiers deployed outside the states don't have access to their bank account until they are back besides is only in the states you can get this card.

ME   I still am not comfortable with spending money on the iTune card instead of my neighbors.

ROD   Hey I see you don't want to talk to me anymore take care and enjoy you life with your neighbors bye

###

This game of playing with a scammer was starting to get boring. Missy wasn't getting anywhere with Rod. He just constantly asked for the stupid iTune card. She was also at a loss for something new to tell him.

The game wasn't going anywhere toward finding any information about him or his location. After all, that was her latest goal and why she continued the game. Hopefully this email was the end. If what he wrote in this last email was true, maybe he had finally given up and moved on. That was okay with her.

But it was not to be. There was a gap of several days and then she got a short and unwanted text message.

ROD   Hi Julie please write me.   I miss you kiss kiss

Chapter 9

What was the strategy of scammers? Do they just wear you down until they finally get what they want? This must be a full-time job for these guys. It would take all day to type out the junk he sends to however many people like her that are dumb enough to respond.

It seemed impossible to get rid of this guy no matter what messages she sent. What else could she do? She could just close out the email address she had created for him and stop the emails. She really hated to drop her cell phone number, as about thirty people had it, and what a pain that would be to set up a message to give out a new number. She wasn't very techy but did think it was possible to block certain incoming numbers, though he could always get a new one and continue texting her.

How was she going to get rid of him? Then she remembered, wait a minute, that wasn't her objective. She had wanted to continue with the communication to keep him busy and maybe learn something useful to locate him. What a dilemma, end the game and never find him or keep it going to get something useful to locate him. Okay she would make one last try and then she would end it for good.

Besides, with the stay-at-home advice, the request to not gather with friends, and the restaurants closing because of the virus Missy was bored. Once again she got out her tablet and drafted a long explicit email to send. It would include asking for direct responses from him and give her proof if he really did pay attention to her emails. She also wanted to get him off the annoying business of asking for the iTune card. Missy waited several days just to get his hopes up and because he made her wait several times.

ME   After your text from yesterday, I was surprised to hear from you. As you know I live alone in a small town. The web is full of dating sites with all sorts of people. There is no way to know who a person really is. You can't really be sure of who I am. With this country in such turmoil, everyone is very cautious.

My friends and neighbors are truly in desperate shape. Even in Iraq I'm sure soldiers are fully aware of the conditions in the US. I hope you can understand why I feel it is more important to use any extra money I have to help my friends with food rather than buy an iTune card for you that you seem to continually ask for. The internet is full of iTune scam alerts - look it up. I wanted to find out if you are really the soldier in the photo you sent. That is why I contacted the army. They will not give out any info on soldiers, so I am at a loss. I would like to remain your friend and continue to communicate, but please don't ask me for anything more than my friendship. Maybe when your service is over and this virus mess is done, we can meet face to face if you want. Until then I will try to be your friend and stay in touch.

Missy was about to congratulate herself on the email she had composed and sent, when days later an email from Rod arrived on her computer. Rod was following suit with her on the delay of several days before responding to each other's emails. He also didn't include anything that corresponded to the email she sent. Maybe she was right, he didn't read her emails or pay attention to what she asked.

ROD   Hi Julie how are you? Sorry I have not been able to communicate with you here I have been very busy here with much responsibility with my team hope all is well with you? How is the virus cases over there? I miss you so much here and please ignore any text from my number I misplaced my cellphone I don't text anymore its only here on email we can communicate. I'm really worried and bothered about you there please protect yourself and stay away from infected victims. Kiss Kiss Emogi Emogi hope to hear from you soon

###

Okay, so the scammer guy wasn't easily prodded for information. How does a person lose a cell phone? All you need to do is have a friend call it and listen for it to ring. At least he was going to email, and she wouldn't have to text on her dumb phone anymore. That was a huge improvement.

The other bonus was he didn't ask about the iTune card. Not one to give up easily, Missy drafted another email. She thought it best to include some virus stuff hoping to deter him from asking for the card. Once again she put in some requests for information still wanting him to tell her something. After a little editing and grammar checks, Missy clicked on send. Now all she would do was wait for a reply.

###

ME   Hi - I thought you had given up on me. I have missed our conversations such as they are with text messages. Email is so much better. Lots to say. The virus thing is crazy. There have been 500 deaths in WA and 10,000 people diagnosed. The economic situation is terrible. So many businesses closed and people out of work. There are very few cars on the road only people walking and riding bikes to get out of their houses and not go nuts. So much for the bad news.

I'm fine and spend my time hiking with my dog and finishing writing my book. I talk to all my friends on the phone and over fences. People are getting so lonely they will stop 6 feet from you just to have a short conversation with a stranger. Our President is fighting with the Governors about starting to open the economy. Oops that's bad news and I'm trying to be positive. Anyway, the sun is shining and it's starting to get warm. The trees are getting their leaves and flowers are blooming. I started getting my garden pots ready and will hopefully have some fresh vegetables this summer.

I hope you are okay and will stay safe. Let me know more about yourself and what your plans are for the future. I'm glad you were able to get back to me.

Another day went by without an email from Rod. Missy knew she was in too deep, because of the way she almost ran to the computer each morning to see if he sent an email. This was beginning to be like a stupid school-girl crush. Wait a minute. This can't be a crush because he's a scammer. Is she mixing up the photo of the soldier with the scammer? That idea has to be crazy. She wondered, if that's crazy, then why hadn't she deleted the photo of the soldier on her phone? Why did this scam interest her so much? Was she really that bored with her life?

She definitely needed to get her life back on track, but how was she going to do that with this virus hanging over everything and everyone? Today she would try to think about other stuff and ignore the computer.

So much for her resolution from the day before. Missy was on her computer first thing the next day looking for a message from Rod. It came at 4:51 AM. Missy Googled Iraq time to see what time he sent the email. It did make some sense with the time difference, but is this what he did when he should be on duty in the middle of the day? Any middle east country would have a time difference too and this could be working hours for scammers.

ROD My love, you are that sweet morning song that plays in my head every morning when i wake up, you are that dream that came true and i cannot begin to express in words, how lucky i feel to have found you and have you in my life, it is you who makes my life complete, and it is you fills my heart with all the wonders and joys of the world. I LOVE YOU

If I'd send you a rose for every time I miss you, you'd be walking in a rose garden.I have never felt this way for anyone, the way I feel for you. It makes me happy, sad, funny, pained and mad, all at the same time. Please don't say that I'm crazy. If I am, it's just for you.Even though I may not say it enough, but I love you with all my heart. You are forever on my mind. They say that true love happens once in a lifetime the cynic in me always doubted that,then i met you and once and for all,i knew that i had to have you in my life,the days that we spend together makes me believe that true love is the kind that happens only once to us and that having that in my life makes me feel like a million bucks , thank you for being there for me every single day,and you love is what keeps us holding,so please don't ever change and continue to love me like this forever. I LOVE YOU hope we can work this out Good morning.

Missy nearly fell off her chair laughing after reading that email. Where did he get that stuff? Some of it seemed like he was typing it from a book or some valentine cards. The grammar was really bad. Obviously he didn't proofread anything and was terrible at typing. It was strange that he didn't put spaces between sentences, and also where he inserted commas. This was another email she had to reread for a second time.

She had hoped for some useful information about the scammer, not a ridiculous bunch of crap about how much he loved her. It also occurred to her that Dotty needed to see her most recent emails. Especially this one.

After reading Rod's ridiculous email for the second time, Missy needed to pay Dotty a visit and let her in on the progression of Rod's 'affection'. This one was so over-the-top that she needed to see Dotty's face when she read it.

Dotty put on the coffee when Missy called to tell her she would be arriving shortly with some juicy emails from Rod. Any ordinary visit with Missy was always a need for coffee, but the promise of more emails made it a must. Not for Missy, it was for Dotty, as she would need the extra caffeine just to keep pace with Missy. Dotty had never met anyone with the energy and enthusiasm that was bottled up in the small package of Missy. Her exuberance was so infectious it lifted Dotty all day.

Just as the coffee pot finished perking, Missy rang the doorbell. Dotty almost broke her ankle zooming to the door. She had been so bored, the promise of juicy emails from Missy's scammer guy was just what she needed.

The scammer messages had entertained her even though she wasn't sure Missy should have kept the game going. Dotty was also surprised how difficult it was becoming to get rid of the scammer. She had agreed with Missy's attempts to get information about the scammer even though they failed.

The excitement was building to see what crazy stuff this scammer guy came up with now. Dotty was polite enough to get Missy coffee before becoming entranced by the emails.

Once again it took Dotty an agonizing amount of time to read the emails, especially the last one. This last full-page scam email she read left her in stitches laughing. Dotty was laughing so hard as she read this 'over-the- top love letter', tears ran down her cheeks.

With a tip of her head and a sly smile Dotty offered, "Isn't he sweet. I think he has a romantic soul."

Missy rolled her eyes, "Dotty, he's a scammer. I doubt he has a soul."

Dotty gave Missy a really sad expression, "I want a scammer who will send me love letters. What was that website you clicked on? Do you think I can get a scammer guy like that too?"

Missy could see Dotty needed to get a life besides hers, "I don't know where he's getting this stuff, but you know it isn't true don't you? Dotty, I think one scammer is enough for the both of us. I can only imagine the type of stuff you would come up with if you got a scammer like this one. The internet would burn up.

I need your help with the kind of response to send back after this last ridiculous email. Give me some ideas for what I can say to get rid of him for good. I know I was going back and forth about wanting to string him along to get information and trying to get rid of him, but the game has to end.

This is getting out of hand with all the love stuff. He has to be a crazy person, not just a scammer. Why would he keep emailing me for all this time without being sent the iTune card?"

"Missy, are you positive you're ready to get rid of this scammer guy?" Dotty asked, knowing how determined a person her friend was about the abuse of the soldier.

Missy didn't really have an answer to Dotty's question. "I'm going home to draft an email response. I'll send it to you first before I send it to Rod. As soon as you read it, call to let me know what you think."

On the drive home Missy again changed her mind about the email she would draft. She knew why Dotty asked her that question. It was because of the soldier, not the scammer. The thought of the real soldier having his identity used entered her mind.

She would keep the scammer busy with the same type of crap he sent her. She would at least be able to keep him busy and away from another unsuspecting little old lady clicking on a photo. Even if the scammer guy was crazy, he was in a third world and couldn't harm her if she was careful. Dotty would be furious, but then she disagreed with most of her ideas.

ME   Hi Rod - Thank you for that wonderful sweet message. I too hope we can one day be together. They say there is such a thing as love at first sight. Unfortunately we only have photos, phone text messages and email conversations. That will have to do for now. To get to know you better and feel close to you, I still would like to know more about you. Your likes and dislikes, your career and what you want in the future.

My life is very happy, but I want someone to share it with. I can imagine lots of fun times to spend together with my best friend. Once again today is sunny and warm. I need to get busy with the flower beds, mowing the lawn and cleaning up the landscape from the winter mess. Soon I will be picking the flowers to put in the house. I moved my horse to a new stable yesterday and will now have lots of new friends to ride with. The goats and chickens are still at my house. This is how I spend my days along with a hike for the dog. I hope your days go well and you can be happy with some of your work. Please stay safe so you can come home.

Chapter 10

Missy 's ears burned with the tirade from Dotty after she read the email that was to be sent to Rod. "What happened between my house and yours? Didn't we agree the game with this scammer had to end?"

"I got to thinking about the soldier and how the scammer is using him," confessed Missy. "It just isn't fair, and I want to torment that creep."

After a skeptical approval from Dotty, Missy sent her email to Rod. Dotty wasn't sure Missy should sound so much like she believed everything in Rod's last email. She did think the email made it clear he needed to tell something about himself.

Dotty began to be just as invested in the scam as Missy and even asked for a copy of the soldier's photo. She also insisted Missy forward all the new emails from Rod to her right way. That wasn't going to work for Missy. She was becoming uncomfortable sending the outrageous emails over the web. Besides, half the fun was seeing the expressions on Dotty's face as she read them. Besides, she needed to keep printing them for her records.

Now Dotty was just as anxious about receiving Rod's emails as Missy.

She was bugging Missy every day for an update on the 'scammer romance', as she put it. Finally, after a delay of three days, an email arrived from Rod.

ROD   How are you? Happy Sunday hope you enjoying your weekend over there? Want you to know I look back on us and I know for a fact that you were all that I needed to truly feel complete. You have fill my life with so many colors that it is hard to keep track of all the joys you bring. Sometimes when you are not aware of it, I look at you and think to myself "How lucky could I possibly be, to have her?" I do not say this to flatter you, but I say this to let you know that love is something that means you now, and it will always be so.

Thanks for the photo you sent me I really appreciate it, and remember you promise to help me this May with the card. Have you receive the money the government promised to give to the citizens I saw some people testifying they have received theirs and it's $1200.

I want you to know that you are always in my heart forever and will continue to be, you are the only woman my heart beats for and will spend the rest of my life with Thanks yours faithfully Rod

Puzzled, Missy wondered how a guy in a third world country would findout about the $1200 checks from the US government? That was something to worry about. Could this be a criminal instead of a typical scammer?

Not only was his next email devoid of any useful information, but he asked for the damn iTune card again. Missy needed to think of an excuse for what she needed to spend her $1200.00 government check on. She was sure Rod would not give up on the card easily now that she and her poor neighbors would have a financial bonus. Time to shut the card request down again.

The disappointment of Rod's unwillingness to come up with any information about himself, and the continuance of asking for the card, was making it difficult for Missy to come up with anything to prompt him. Instead she would put in some miscellaneous stuff. It took her a couple days to get inspired again.

###

ME Hi - Sorry to get back to you so late. I had a busy day - worked on my book, played with my horse and hiked with my dog. Just didn't have time to sit down at the computer. Last night a friend came over with two pieces of salmon for me to cook. That took a while as I didn't know how to cook it. I'll fore warn you - I don't know how to cook. I can make a good spaghetti, stew, cottage pie, bake chicken breasts and now broil salmon. Other than that I buy prepared stuff at Costco. I do, however, bake the best cookies ever. Those are my only talents in the kitchen.

As far as the government check, that will go to pay property tax that is due April 30. So much for free money. I still can't send you the card you want. I will try to get more photos on my computer and send them. Right now I'm going to get my glass of wine and watch something on the TV. Please stay safe and return home soon. I can't wait to be able to talk in person.

Julie, your new best friend.

The next afternoon another failed email came from Rod.

ROD How are you doing today Julie? Sorry for the late reply

I hope this virus is ending soon.   Hope you your day is going well over there? Why did you say you can't send me the card by May as you promised

Wish you a nice and blissful day ahead

Missy put in a call to Dotty wanting her advice for a way to get Rod off the card requests. Dotty was now getting bored with the scammer game. The bloom of romance was gone, and the reality of the unsuccessful scam was lurking over her too. Missy wasn't sure it was the virus atmosphere or the lack of success with scamming Rod back, but both she and Dotty were losing interest.

Missy was at a loss for ideas, "Dotty, what do you think we can do to get him to reveal himself?"

Dotty had the answer, "Missy, why don't you try to put more doom and gloom in an email. Make him feel sorry for you. That's what he's trying to do to you."

Missy had another thought, "I'm beginning to think he never reads my emails. I think he just sends out the same crap to the many dumb women he has on the hook. If I don't get anywhere soon, I'm going to give up. I'll forward you the next reply email to him with a lot of doom and gloom as you put it. I'm not sure this is worth the effort, but I'll give it one last try."

71

Missy went home with a bit of depression about the virus and Rod. She composed the email and clicked on send.

###

ME   Today is a cold and gloomy day. I decided to try to finish my novel since I would rather be inside where it is warm. This virus thing is not going away. Today I noticed even more restrictions at Walmart. The isles are labeled 'one way' and there are squares all over the isle floors indicating for people to stay 6' away from each other. There are so many people filing for unemployment that the system is failing. The small business administration has run out of money for business loans. Sorry for all the doom and gloom, but this is how it is. The virus cases on the area have leveled off as we are quite isolated and people from the other areas are not coming over.   I'm probably fairly safe here.

I still am concerned about money and our economy is in such dire shape. I only spend money on bare necessities. Sorry, but I don't feel I can get you the card you want. Please only ask me for my friendship as I can freely give you that.

###

Another email came from Rod that definitely was causing Missy to lose interest. It was clear Rod didn't read her emails. He must be a professional scammer. This email proved it. Where was he getting this crap? Since the spelling and grammar had improved, it was obvious he was copying it from somewhere, and he had a Bible. That seemed

72

really low for a scammer to quote from the Bible. Does he think by implying he's religious it will make him more believable?

What he put in the email would be lovely if it was from the soldier in the photo, but it only angered Missy. Especially the very last sentence. She would try one last time to end the card requests. It would be a very direct email.

ROD   Hello Julie - I want you to know Love is patient, love is kind. It does not envy, it does not boast, it is not proud. It does not dishonor others, it is not self-seeking, it keeps no record of wrongs. Love does not delight in evil but rejoices with the trust. It always protects, always trusts, always hopes, and always perseveres. Love never fails, but where there are prophecies, they will cease; where there are tongues, they will be stilled; where there is knowledge, it will pass away. For we know in part and we prophesy in part, but when completeness comes, what is in part disappears. When I was a child, I talked like a child, I thought like a child, I reasoned like a child. When I became a man, I put the ways of childhood behind me. For now we see only a reflection as in a mirror; then we shall see face to face. Now I know in part; then I shall know fully, even as I am fully known.

And now these three remain: faith, hope and love. But the greatest of these is love..1 Timothy 1:5 says that "Love comes from a pure heart and a good conscience and a sincere faith. Ecclesiastes 4:9-12 says that two are better than one, because they have a good return for their work: If one falls down, his friend can help him up. But pity the man who falls and has no one to help him up! Also, if two lie down together, they will keep warm. But how can one keep warm alone? The one may be overpowered, two can defend themselves For all this I see the importance of you in my life and realized that my years of waiting to find the right woman, worth it. Romans 8:28 says: "And we know that all things work together for good to them that love God, to them who are called according to his purpose". Ecclesiastes 3:1 says, "To everything there is a season, and a time to every purpose under the heavens". I feel like this is my season. I have already asked God in prayers to separate us if we are not meant to be but it seems we are meant to be because I have come to realize that each time I have my private moment that I always think of you. Why did you say you can't send me the card as promised?

ME   You continually ask me for the card. If we truly have a sincere relationship, my not sending you the card is of little consequence. I have tried to explain the serious situation here due to the virus. The welfare of my friends and neighbors is more important to me than sending you a card. If you cannot understand that, I'm not sure you are the person I hope you are. Please discontinue asking me as I cannot respond to your request. I only want to be your friend and keep you company with my emails.

Chapter 11

Just as Missy decided Rod never read her emails, one came that changed everything. It was time to go big or go home. She could end this scam, or she had a chance to move on and get the information she wanted on the scammer. It took Missy all day to compose the perfect email to sink the hook into Rod.

###

ROD   Hello How are you doing today Julie? Hope all is well with you? Please stay safe and protect yourself from the infected victims...I want as you this question and I need a sincere answer What do you think about me? Do you ever think this relationship will work? Do you have feelings for me?

ME   I am fine and busy finishing my book. I think it is finally done. The isolation of the 'stay at home' and social distancing thing is getting old. It is difficult knowing you cannot get close to anyone. I miss a hug once in a while. I have friends at the barn to talk to which helps and one really close friend I talk to daily. She is getting older and I make sure she is okay. My animals keep me busy too. It is getting more and more difficult to even hike with my dog as all the city, county, state and federal parks are closed.

I'm not sure what to think of you as I don't know very much about you. I would like to know you better-things you like or dislike, do you like animals, have had any and do you want to have some, what you want for your future, things you have done in the past, places you have lived or want to live.

I certainly want to have feelings for you as I enjoy our conversations. It is difficult to know if you love someone that you don't know anything about. The only thing you have told me is that you were an orphan, have a daughter and were married. I like the poetic emails you send. I hope they are truly from your heart. I want to have a physical and emotional relationship with a man that will last forever. I would like that you could be the man. I want more than an email relationship. I want to talk with and touch the man who will spend the rest of his life with me. I'm a very open and honest type of person and need that from my best friend who will be with me forever.

I have come to look forward to corresponding with you and want us to be closer. I hope we can accomplish this.

Very truly yours, Julie

###

Missy was finally feeling like she was getting somewhere. Time would tell if this last email to Rod would have the effect she wanted. She was afraid this could backfire and this scam would become all too real. What if he continued with all the romantic emails? Could she keep her feelings for the soldier separate from the scammer?

There wasn't a man currently in her life and she was a bit lonely at times during the pandemic. It would be so nice to have someone special to hug. It was now more important than ever to keep in mind this guy was only a scammer, and she was playing a game. Missy kept telling herself - stop being so anxious for his replies to my emails. This is an evil criminal who sends those messages. When the next email came from Rod, success had happened.

###

ROD   Hello How are you? How is your day going over there I want you to know am a simple individual and am always eager to meet new friends and get along with them. I do not smoke but drink occasionally. i enjoy all kinds of music and i love to dance. My friends says am easy going person and have such a warm sense of humor. i love pets even though i don't have. How i spend my weekends, i usually go for Zumba Zumba dance here.its one of the traditional dance and maybe someday if nature allows us and we get along very well, hopefully we meet....i will take you with me on my dancing class. I love to read too and mostly novels that are interesting.such as "First Night" etc....what is your experience so far. i will stop here until i receive a letter from you. have a nice day

Missy gave herself a big girl talk and decided to go all out on the next email. She would give him some of the most intimate feelings she could come up with. As she prepared the email text, it occurred to her that what she was drafting for this email was close to her own heart. The things she was describing sounded all too wonderful. How great it would be to have a man in her life that she could feel this way about. What a waste to give these thoughts to a creep like this scammer. Could she ever have this with someone for real? The photo of the soldier popped into her head. Would he be the type of a man worthy of what she was about to send to the scammer?

"Stop it, stop it," she said to herself. "This is a game I'm playing. This is not how I will find my prince charming. Rod is a scammer whom I dislike intensely. I have to keep my life separate from this stupid thing I'm doing with this scammer."

Missy wrote her next email and thought, 'Okay, Rod take this and go with it.'

#

ME   Hi Glad to hear from you. Thank you for letting me know more about yourself. I think we would get along great. I start my day early and go full throttle until evening with a glass of wine and relaxing. Most of my day is playing with and caring for my animals and visiting with friends. I don't dance much as I don't have a partner. I used to dance, especially like slow dance with soft music. I too like music. I'm not sure about Zumba as I have not seen it. I like to read murder mysteries that have a lot of intrigue.   I'm not a religious or overly spiritual person, but I do believe in fate.

These are the things that are important to me - Staying close to your friends, walking on the beach with your best friend holding hands, a snuggle with your best friend as a perfect end to the day, the look on your face that says you're all I will ever need and want, a spontaneous compassionate gesture, the ability to laugh at yourself and wanting to give more than receive. I hope these things mean something to you as well.

Hope your day goes well and stay safe, Julie.

#

Once again it was time to visit with Dotty and get her view of Rod and his emails. Missy clicked on the forward button and sent Rod's latest email and her response email to Dotty. Hopefully Dotty would have read it by the time she arrived at her house.

Dotty answered the door with her opinion after reading the emails, "Well, you have done it now. You've finally gone too far. This is getting way too serious. I hope you haven't fallen for the stupid stuff he sends. I don't know how you come up with the stuff you're sending him. Where do you see this scheme of yours going?"

"Wow you really said a mouthful there," replied Missy not truly letting her thoughts be known. "I'm keeping my perspective on track. You don't honestly think I could be taken in by this guy? I know he's a scammer and a crook. I'm just trying to get some information. Maybe if he thinks I'm serious, he will let his guard down. Don't worry, I know what I'm doing and won't get in too deep."

"I would certainly hope not," was Dotty's response, although from the tone of her voice she was not convinced. "I still feel this project of yours is dangerous. How can you be sure he's in some third world country? There are ways to trace people these days. You yourself know how the 'smart' devices track everything people do. It's possible he could find you and maybe thinks he could get more from you than just that card he wanted."

"I promise to be careful. Don't worry I have my head on straight." Missy knew Dotty had her best interests at heart and headed home without any further lectures.

Missy was fairly sure she was safe from the scammer and not in any type of danger. She had to keep this scheme as Dotty called it in perspective. The only danger was starting to feel something when she read the next email from Rod that was truly getting too serious. Missy was starting to wish the words from Rod were from the soldier. The longer this game went on the more difficult it was to separate the two.

It took several days to get a response from her last email to Rod which came at the unusual hour of 2:10 AM. Missy got more than she bargained for in the next email from Rod.

No wonder it took so long for him to send this email. What really surprised her was the content. It appeared he was not sending a prepared script, and somewhat followed her last email. He was still a bit over the top with his romantic expressions. Now he was asking her for even more personal information that she was definitely not going to give.

One thing about the email did stand out. The spelling and punctuation were better than usual. She wondered if this could be a standard format each scammer used. It was true to the email she had just sent, but still generic in nature. All these slight changes in the scammers emails was quite confusing to Missy. This was a very unusual scammer.

###

ROD   Dear babe how are you babe? I think you are an amazing woman that could change my life forever. You can trust in me. I can not tell you how important our relationship is and where I would like it to go. Although we have been friends for the last couple of weeks I feel there is a real connection between us. You can allow me into your heart to love you completely. I am not here to try to hurt you because you are a wonderful friend. I just want to share my world with you - and I hope you feel the same..You have been the sweetest, most understanding person I have ever needed. It's hard to believe how much we have been through lately but I promise you the best future ever and I owe my entire life to you. You are my inspiration everyday and I wake up every morning thinking of how wonderful it would be to wake up with you. Do you feel there is a chance that we can be together in the future? Sorry to seem so forward. I am very thankful to know someone like you. Sometimes I wonder if you feel the same about me that we will be together very soon. i like the way you talk to me with care, listen to everything I have to say] and it is an amazing feeling to get such attention. Your sense of adventure intrigues me as well as captured my full attention. I am thankful to have a woman who enjoys the beauty our world has to offer. Did you know it was one of the best attributes of your character? You appreciate invaluable moments and it makes me appreciate you even more. I love the way we are growing together. The incredible conversations, trips, and dates in exotic places is just too overwhelming with a common mind. You have helped me expand my horizons in so little time. At this very moment, I am thinking of your smile and what lies ahead.

I want to spend the rest of my life with you. No one can ever take your place because there isn't a person like you in the world. Please let me love you. i know you will be accepting me with all your heart. I do notice every little thing you do. This feeling is always present when I think of you. If you think we can move forward, could you please let me know what's on your mind? I want to learn more about you - your fears, aspirations, and passions. I want to listen to your heartbeat at night before I go to bed. I hear your voice in my head when things are going rough. Please stay the same throughout our days together. I know that we will change in the future, but lets change together. Lets stay in the moment of what we have...and work on the future we want. We can do anything we want to do if we keep ourselves on the same accord. I know that you will be there with me

Love you always.

Hook, line, and sinker. Was this really what Missy wanted? Could she actually get the scammer to reveal something useful? If Rod was a professional scammer, the task would be difficult. She would need to continue matching his emails with the same kind of devotion the last one expressed. She needed to ask for what she really wanted: information that would lead to his exposure and maybe stop him from scamming people. Was stopping him even possible? He could be alone or part of a huge operation. There was only one way to find out - keep the scam going.

Missy was eager to find out Dotty's thoughts about this elaborate email from Rod and her reply email. She had been printing them, driving to Dotty's house for her to read, but this was too exciting for a wait that long. The entertainment value of these emails was over the top. Missy opened the file and pressed - send.

ME   Rod - I am completely overwhelmed by your last email. Yes, I too want us to be together forever. I know if we were together, I would love you as much as you love me. You have poured your heart out to me and I am beyond pleased you are able to do that. A man able to feel the things you have revealed is all I could hope for and want to spend the rest of my life with.

You have said before that you intend to retire from the service. What do you want to do with the rest of your life and what do you think the future will hold for us? I would so much want for us to meet, get to know each other better and see what our future would be like. Please let me know if and when this could be possible. I want you in my life for real and not just in my computer.

Please let me be in your life and love you - Julie

Missy's phone rang and it showed Dotty's name. Evidently, Dotty had read the last emails she forwarded to her. Missy could only imagine the scolding she was about to receive. She was right, and Dotty let her have it.

"I had no idea you could be such a romantic and an idiot. The crap you come up with is just as stupid as the crap from Rod. This has to be by far the most ridiculous thing you have ever done. I don't even know you anymore. What do you think sending an email like that to this scammer guy will accomplish?"

"Just what I have wanted all along," explained Missy. "I want to expose this guy and stop him from scamming people. If I keep the game going maybe I can get him to let something slip that will lead to his location and who he's working for."

Dotty was emphatic, "You need to stop this right now. That's a job for the FBI or somebody like that. What if he's part of some mob? Those people don't play games, they kill people."

Missy had to laugh imagining the stern look on Dotty's face. "Don't you think that's a little over dramatic? I doubt this guy or anyone he works for puts that kind of effort into people like me. They just keep after lonely old ladies until they get some money or whatever they're after. Sooner or later, he will give up if I don't send him what he wants and move on. Let's just see where it goes for a little longer."

Dotty's voice now sounded threatening, "Just promise me this is the last email like that you send him. If this game doesn't end soon, I'll shoot you myself. I don't know about you, but my stress level is going to give me a heart attack."

Chapter 12

The next day Missy got the email from Rod that she was expecting. He was moving off the requests for the card and onto something bigger. This was a hint that he might want her to help him invest in a business. Was this what scammers do? Get control of the victim and squeeze for a huge payoff.

She would try to move away from this aspect and continue with the romance. Being able to work her side of the scam involving any type of business venture wasn't a possibility she could handle. If that was his game now, it would probably end before she reached her objective. She reread his email to give her some ideas of what to say next.

ROD   Hi sweetie how are you? Sorry I couldn't write you back on time I have been very busy with much responsibility with my team, Yes I will retire soon thank God I found you all I wish for is a woman I will spend the rest of my life enjoy my old age with her because I have worked and laboured for years I need to live life to the fullest with my partner look for a very lucrative business and invest on. From the day we met I said to myself that this is the woman my heart beats for and accepts am happy we have been able to communicate and know more about each other let's plan on how we gonna live if you ready to relocate, what business to you thing will be good and profitable. Once again thanks for coming into my life I really appreciate and remain grateful to God for bringing you my way. Have a blessed day Kiss emogi kiss emogi kiss emogi

Missy sent an email that completely related to Rod's, was short, and to the point. If that was his game now, what she wrote would probably insure she couldn't handle his request. Her response also had to continue asking personal questions.

ME   Thanks for your email and letting me know your future plans. I really like where I live and am not really interested in relocating. Where are you planning to live? I don't know anything about business or investments, so I am no help to you in that regard. I just want your friendship and companionship for a happy life together. You would have to give me more information about your future plans for me to understand what you want.

Your friend Julie

Since the latest emails were a bit more generic, Missy decided to forward them to Dotty. After about fifteen minutes for Dotty to read the emails, Missy picked up the phone and called her. "Hi, what do you think of the last email from Rod and my response to him?"

Minus the usual scolding, Dotty told her, "I still don't know why you're messing with this guy, but you may be right. He's moving on to get a bigger payday. It will be interesting to see if you're successful in ending his quest for a business investment. If that's what he's after, maybe you should give him a hint you don't have any money."

Dotty now had a tone of concern in her voice, "I know you want to find something about him, but please try not to get in so deep. You promised me that you would keep this game under control."

Missy had the same concerns, "I'll try to stay anonymous and send you the next emails. Then we can decide where to go from there."

Rod's next email came at the unusual hour of 7:35 PM. His emails usually came before dawn or early in the morning. Luckily Missy had her computer on and decided to email right back with a like kind email.

ROD   Hi Julie...I got your email I must tell you this, if am welcomed and accept am not worried about anything else I love adventure, well I have to tell you that I have made up my mind to relocate and spending the rest of my life with you. But you have to promise something promise me you will always stand by me no matter any circumstances? You and I is now one body I believe we have to be open with each other share our moments as lover and the most important thing again earn how to trust, respect and believe one another, Thanks.

ME   The only thing I can say is I hope that when we finally meet face to face our feelings for each other will capture the moment and seal our relationship. You will be welcomed into my life and love. Trust and respect are things that grow as two people become one. We have already had some rough moments, but have never given up on one another. I'm a simple woman living on a small income and quiet life. There must be something in the universe that has brought us together and will hopefully keep us together. Nothing and no one is ever perfect. You just have to work to find the best in each other and accept it. I want to share my life with the most important person in my world - my best friend who loves me as much as I love him. I want the person who sends me the lovely emails to be my best friend.

Stay by me Rod - Julie

Five days went by without an email from Rod. Missy had started to think Rod was working an angle to get more money from her. He must have given up when she put the sentence in saying she had a small income. Oh well, she tried. She knew from the beginning the only thing he really wanted was money, not love. It was a game they were playing and maybe it had come to an end. Life would go back to normal and maybe she would start another novel. Some ideas were floating around in her head. Missy opened her computer after lunch intending to start on an outline for the next novel when an email alert popped up.

ROD   Hi Julie How are you doing? I'm sorry I couldn't write you back on time hope all is well with you happy military appreciation month..

Happy New month wish yo a nice and blissful month I really miss you here hope to meet with you soon take care love you and hope to hear from you positively

###

Well, so much for losing touch with Rod. He was back, but it was fairly short, and she had no idea it was military appreciation month. Even stranger, how would a scammer know that? The new novel would have to be put on the back burner for the moment. She needed an email that would rekindle their relationship and get him to reveal what is going on with him.

###

ME   Hi - I worry when I don't hear from you for a while. Hope you are okay and haven't had any problems. I'm doing fine, just getting tired of this virus thing. Miss my friends as I can only talk with them on the phone and not in person. Seems strange not being able to go anywhere. I have friends at the barn and we are not really doing the social distancing thing since we are outdoors. At least we can talk to each other face to face. I really like people and miss hugs.

Enough of the bad stuff. We have had some nice afternoons and I've been able to take the dog on hikes. There is only one trail I like that is open, and it's pretty with the river on one side and fields with cows on the other. It takes an hour to walk from one end to the other which is fine. The trees are getting leaves and looking better. I should be outside working on my flower beds and plucking weeds, but I can't get away from my computer and working on my new book. It's raining today, so the book will win out. They say the parks and golf courses will open at the end of the week. I hope so, better hiking trails and I could use some practice on the driving range.

That's how my life is going for now. I know it would be better with you in it. Hope that will be soon. Be careful and stay safe for me. Julie

Chapter 13

Two days went by without an email from Rod and Missy was again starting to think he had decided to move on. Maybe she should have put something more romantic or ask for inquiring stuff in her last email. Dotty would be relieved that the scam was over.

Another problem came to her. How was she going to entertain Dotty now? It would be very difficult to top the stupid scam. Oh well, now she could get back to her life since the scam was likely over.

Just like before, after a delay another afternoon email arrived from Rod. This one confirmed the end of her crazy scammer game. She guessed this was the most logical way for him to end the scam since he was impersonating a soldier.

###

ROD   Hi Julie How are you doing over there my love? Hope all is well with you? I really really miss you here but try to understand the nature of my work I have been very busy with my team here as am among the soldiers short listed for a raiding all I need is your prayers it's a very difficult and risky one suicide mission. Even if you did not hear from again just bare it in mind that you are always in my heart both in death. Once again thanks for your kindness and wonderful hand of love I love you so much kiss emogi kiss emogi kiss.

What Missy needed was an email that sounded sincere, but also left the future open if he didn't 'die' in the suicide mission, whatever that was. No use going to much effort if the scam was ending. It was such a relief to write her last email. She just put in something simple.

ME   Hi - I'm fine, but now you have me worried. Your mission sounds scary. Please be careful and stay safe. I will wait anxiously for your email telling me you are okay. The county park near my house opened and I hiked with my dog there yesterday and today. It is my favorite trail as it runs above the ocean and through a forest.

Stay safe and come home to me. Julie

###

So much for fantasy land. She forwarded the last two emails to Dotty who would be thankful the scam ended. For several weeks her email file was devoid of messages from Rod. Missy's scam escapade was over, and her normal life was back. She headed over to Dotty's house so they could reminisce about her silly cyber romance with a scammer. They both laughed over a couple cups of coffee and decided Missy was better off now that it was over. Secretly, Missy's only problem was regretting that she would no longer have thoughts of the soldier.

Missy brought copies of her new novel's pages to share with Dotty. From now on they would concentrate on this novel and how it was going to evolve. This was a far better and safer type of entertainment.

It was spring and the days were getting longer and bright. That always makes everything better, but Missy still had a deep lingering feeling of loss for the soldier in the photo. He would never know that she would look at the photo on her phone and secretly want to know him.

Weeks went by without any further emails from Rod. Missy was starting to forget about the scam and focused on her new novel. As she went to the kitchen to start dinner she had some very intriguing ideas pop into her head about one of the characters. Whenever this happened it was best to go to her desk and write it down before the thoughts left her. This character was a nice handsome man, and his vision was now on her mind and taking the place of the soldier. As she added her thoughts about this character into the computer an email alert popped up.

When she looked to see who it was from, she felt a sudden surge of excitement. It was from Rod. How stupid she was to be excited about the scam returning. She was supposed to move on with her life, not be happy he survived his mission.

ROD   HELLO DEAR, Thank your for your prayers and also your email, I missedyou so much and I am so sorry for keeping you waiting honey, your thought saved my life today. Our van got hit by RPG, the power turned it over and I took a bullet. We got pinned down and there was no exit, through out the 1 hour 30mins there was sound of bullets all through this moment,i was face to face with death I never paused thinking about you. There was heavy firing and we secured a safe position till our back up came to our rescue, I wanted to live to see another day for and with you. I am OK, but a bullet was on my right leg, honey there is nothing to worry about, it is just a flesh cut. At least now I will be out of action for at least a week, I took a walk to the command room just to send this email and to inform you that I am well You don't know how crazy I am for you already,

During our raiding and bursting of these bastards [talibans terrorist] our Intel passed a resourceful information to us and with the lead our base approved we made the confrontation and to greatest surprise we found in their hide-out lots of ammunitions. it was a plan for a suicide plot against our base and a huge amount of cash in US dollars. These people are terrible, how can a human being sit and plan to kill his fellow human being just because of his belief and it is so unbelievable. On our way back to the camp we made a stop and our Commander summoned myself and 2 other Team captains like myself, he mapped out some of the money we found in their base for our well being as a compensation. I can't say no, I took it with the reality of the fact that I will be leaving the Army soon. I remembered so many good comfort the money will provide when I leave the Army, I took it and we took an oath of secrecy with the commander and the other team captains like me. I have with me as I am sending this mail the sum of $2.8m US dollars as my share, Two million and Eight hundred thousand US dollars, my fear is that this money cannot be safe in the camp because we are not allowed to keep cash. Honey, when I write this message, I am proud of $ 2.8 million dollars (two million and eight hundred thousand US dollars) We know that this can not be safe, here in our camp. The inspection team in camp they can confiscate the money Who do I send it to? who can I trust to keep it for me? my love now i know fate brought us together for a purpose. I strongly believe in my heart that we are made for each other, I keep asking myself why now? I just have less than 2 months to leave the Army, and now I am in love with you. My love, from the moment the bag of money was handed over to me and the question of who will keep this for me, that moment your thought came into my mind. I nursed no fear and I felt no doubt. I believe that it will be safe with you and there won't be any problem, all you need to do is receive this money and safe keep it until I come over. I know that we belong together and if you accept me as your sweet husband then this money will provide good comfort for us. Do not say a word about this to anyone; the only problem will be when you tell people because they will want to steal the money from you by all means. My love, would you safe guide the money for us? our medical supply will be coming in any moment from now. All I need to do is to hand over the money to him who is the red cross man, which I have carefully wrapped in an ultra violet material and safely placed in a metal box used for our medical supply the red cross that clears our medical supply to lift it out of our base. please let me have you FULL NAME,......ADDRESS..... TELEPHONE NUMBER,......EMAIL ADDRESS.....My love, when will you be on line, I need us to chat for long. I love you so much my true love. Please tell me when you will be on line because I will wait online for you because this isvery important to me,i am in pain now but i will do my best to connect with you for a chat so that you will get a better understanding please send me you Name and address where it will be delivered to and remember not to tell any body about now and after the delivery. LOVE ALWAYS, YOUR HUSBAND ROD STODDARD.

###

As Missy read this unbelievable email from Rod, she laughed so hard tears ran down her cheeks and splashed on the keyboard. Once again she had to

reread the lengthy email again and again to grasp everything he said. He must have been in the cube he worked from for quite a while to compose all this.

One thing was crystal clear, he wanted to know where she lived. The truly evil side of this scammer had come to light. So much for a loving husband to be. Missy's laughter stopped realizing Dotty was right, she was in danger.

How could she consider continuing the scam now that he wanted her location. The thought of a scammer coming to her house was terrifying. She lived alone and there wasn't anyone to protect her.

A picture suddenly popped into her head. It was of the soldier in the photo on her phone. It was stupid thinking he would protect her from the scammer who now seemed threatening. One thing was for sure, she would never send her address to Rod. This new scenario was so incredible, even though scary, she wanted to see where he would go next. Was he playing a game with her like the one she was playing?

A very careful response was needed to remain out of danger. She would have to think of an alternative for him sending the money, which surely didn't exist anyway. Missy had a lot to think about and bouncing her ideas off Dotty would help. This email didn't seem safe to be floating on the web, so she would print it and not forward to Dotty.

She wondered how many cups of coffee would be consumed during the discussion of Rod's latest email. She wouldn't need her car to get home, she would be hyped enough on coffee to fly home.

Dotty took forever and a full cup of coffee to read and assimilate Rod's email. Unlike Missy, Dotty didn't laugh as she read. "I knew something like this would happen. How stupid does this guy think people are? Why would someone think a soldier in the army could get that kind of money from a raid. Why would he think someone would believe it could be sent to them? If this is a standard scam method used; I'd be shocked if it ever worked. I think he's tired of the game you have been playing and is calling your bluff."

Missy could see Dotty came to the same conclusion she did. "Dotty you're absolutely right, I would never in a million years guess he would come up with something this outrageous. I have one more play up my sleeve and then I'm going to end this for good."

Missy stood and prepared to leave, "I'll forward you my reply to his email when I get home. I'm going to keep it short and not give much mention to the money."

###

ME   Hi - I don't know what to say about all this. I'm glad you're not seriously injured and hope you will heal soon. I'm not as comfortable about the money. If you want it okay. We will have to talk about that when you get out of the Army. My address is not secure enough for something like this. I will need to get a post office box. I'll let you know when I have accomplished it.

Within minutes Missy received a reply email from Rod.

ROD   Hi sweetie how are you? Hope all is well with you? I want to thank you very much for your prayers I believe it's what saved me here when I went for this mission I really appreciate and miss you so much Emogi

Please I really need you to send me the details I listed above cuz this money is not safe here so I can send it to you as soon as possible before the inspection team will come to the camp OK

I love you more and more I very have an spending the rest of my life with a woman that her heart is full of love and care, I must confess I love you yesterday today tomorrow and forever.

Please send me your cellphone number email address home address so I can send this parcel to you as soon as possible delay is dangerous Thanks hope to hear from you positively kiss emogi kiss emogi

Rod if nothing else was a persistent scammer. He must have a lot of time on his hands. How many people does a scammer have in his portfolio at one time? Missy was not going to waste much effort as this scam would probably end very soon. She was busy with her novel and wanted to put the scam aside. Evidently scammers want immediate replies. Rod sent another email at an unusual time, 11:37 PM. Missy read the email the next morning when she opened her computer and sent a reply.

ROD   Hi Julie how are you? What is going on with you? Hope all is well with you? I have been waiting for your reply but you are silent, like I told you earlier others have sent theirs home and I'm avoiding the inspection team to see it, this is what I have achieved and laboured for please sweetie understand me and send me what is needed is soon as possible OK. Thanks

ME   I still need to get a post office box as my mailbox is not near my house and can be vandalized. That is my only option.

###

Missy had hoped the necessity for a post office box was a solution, but that was not to be. The next day another email came from Rod. He was a bit sharper than she had anticipated. She would have to come up with something else. Her idea would have to work, or this would need to be the end.

###

ROD   Hi sweetie how are you? Please understand me, send me your address: name : email address phone number, it gonna be delivered to you direct to your door step. So I can go to the delivery company to send it to you as soon as possible delay is dangerous. Thank hope to hear from you positively.

ME   I'm not home much and it would not be safe to leave anything at my door step. Packages are stolen from doorsteps all the time. You will have to think of something else.

###

The next email from Rod really gave Missy something to be afraid of. If she was dumb enough to send him her address, not only would he know where she lived, but someone could actually show up. Rod was determined to get her address. It was also clear he wasn't a very sophisticated scammer. He should be able to do a Google search with her phone number or email address and get her physical home address. How far was he willing to go?

ROD   Hi Julie how are you? Wish you a nice and blissful day ahead. Regarding to the message you sent please send me the details and your city once the parcel arrives to your city they gonna call you and know when you are home to deliver the parcel...Like I told you earlier delay is dangerous do you want me to lose what I have achieved and laboured for send me your cellphone number city email address. Hope to here from you positively thanks

Fright was an understatement when Missy thought about what she had gotten herself into. This scam definitely had to end and end now. The odd thing was he continually requested her phone number which he should have since he sent her text messages to it. Also, he kept requesting her email address which was strange too since he just sent an email to her.

Maybe there was more than one person involved in this scam. Has this scam been moved up the chain to someone else? Could the messages even be computer generated? She would not reply to this last email and would make sure her doors were locked at all times. Missy even considered buying a gun but was afraid she would shoot her foot or something else.

Several days went by without any emails or text messages from Rod. Missy was feeling a little safer. Dotty had stopped admonishing her for playing this crazy game with a scammer. She was sitting at her computer one afternoon when her cell phone made the one sound she feared the most - a text message had come through.

ROD   It is very important for me to express to you how much you really mean to me. I wish I could do this in person while holding you in my arms and gazing into your eyes. But since we are physically separated by miles of emptiness, this expression must come in the form of letters such as this. Babe, I know it is difficult for you, as it is for me, to be separated for so long. Life seems to be full of trials of this type which test our inner strength, and more importantly, our devotion and love for one another. After all, it is said that "True Love" is boundless and immeasurable and overcomes all forms of adversity. In truth, if it is genuine, it will grow stronger with each assault upon its existence. One that will share my sorrows with me and one that will be there for me in terms of good and problems. You see, there are also a degree sequential. I may choose first TRUST AND COMMUNICATION. They go hand in hand and without them any type of relationship; business, personal, family, whatever, is bound to fail. Good morning Happy New month Rod Stoddard

Missy's hands were shaking as she read the text message. Why would he send something like this? Also, why a text message this long instead of an email. It took forever to scroll through her dumb phone to read it. All of his previous emails had been all about the money. Now, why did he send a text message with all the romantic love crap. This text message, which was surprisingly long, must have been copied since the spelling and punctuation was better than his normal text messages and emails. Maybe this text message was on his phone from before the money text messages and he accidentally sent it. Anyway, it was not going to make any difference. She was finished with Rod and didn't reply back. Hopefully, he would give up and end the scam. Two days later an email came that again sent shivers up her spine.

###

ROD   Hi Julie how are you? Happy New Month I sent you message on your cellphone number you ignored it, I must tell you that you are not acting like someone who have a good and human heart you know where I am and things am passing through here you don't show any sign of care even if we have not met before but I'm here serving the nation the little care you will all you do is to give me excuses. I'm writing this email to you I see you don't believe me am gonna surprise you drop me your home address whenever I'm back in the state I pay you a surprising visit thanks Stoddard hope to hear from you positively

Chapter 14

Missy had to think of something that would keep Rod from trying to find her. Especially something to make him think it would not be safe to confront her. He knew she lived alone and that made her vulnerable. She needed reinforcements to get this guy to leave her alone, so she went to get some much-needed advice from her ally, Dotty.

Missy and Dotty put their heads together. What would make this guy give up on the scam? He wasn't getting any money and Missy hadn't sent her address. What was he after? He was more than persistent, he almost seemed obsessed. That concept was even more frightening than the stuff he wrote in the emails. What she needed was a man in her life to protect her. One like the soldier in the photo on her phone. If only he were real.

"Dotty, what is it going to take to get rid of him?" Missy let her inner feeling slip, "I wish I had a guy for protection like the soldier."

"Missy, you've been overly interested in the soldier in the photo. He doesn't have anything to do with this scam. It's likely he doesn't even know his identity is being used by the scammer."

Dotty could see this was a problem. This terrible outcome from the scam must be very confusing for her, thought Dotty. "The soldier might not be real either. There is such a thing as photoshop too. That could be an old photo of a soldier, or he could even, God forbid, have been killed in action and not even be alive. You need to get off the idea of the soldier and onto some other man. Let's compose an email with a solution to end this scam and send it today."

They decided a dear John letter might do the trick. Missy didn't need to elaborate but could use the excuse of the time Rod was away on his suicide mission. The wording would have to be strong and convincing. Missy decided on a text message instead of an email for the dear John letter.

ME   Hi Rod - I met someone during your suicide raid. I'm getting married. He's a wonderful and very protective man. Have to say goodbye. Hope you understand.

###

Four days went by, and Missy once again was thinking the scam was over.

Wrong, an email came that was completely off base. At least he didn't ask for her address, but still mentioned coming to see her.

ROD   Hi Julie how are you? Hope all is well with you over there? I want you to know that my feelings is natural and I promise to see you once am in the State I have been very busy here went for a special duty that is why I have not contacted you please e safe and take good care of yourself I really miss you here on chat kiss emogi emogi kiss emogi emogi and hope to hear from you positively thanks.

Where did this come from? Was it another case that he had something ready to send and hadn't gotten her dear john letter text message before he sent this? Regardless, Missy was done with Rod and would continue trying to end the scam. Was his promise to see her when he returned to the states only to keep her in the scam? Still she thought there could be an answer to that question. She drafted a very short email and sent it.

###

ME   When will you return to the US? Let's see what happens when you get back.

###

Before Missy could turn the computer power off an email came from Rod. At least this answered her question as to whether he received her dear john letter text message.

###

ROD   Hi Julie thank for your email, if is in my powers I will be home as soon as possible...Please I need your sincere answer on this have seen another man or you just want to use it to scare me away, am really interested in you as seeing my future with you. Please tell me my stand and faith in you I can't afford to lose you. Thanks and hope to hear from you positively.

###

Now that she was sure he got the dear john letter, she would have to make him believe it. It was time to sit down with Dotty again and come up with a better strategy.

Dotty had more ideas, "You have certainly gotten yourself into a mess now. That wasn't much of a dear john letter. Maybe the text message was too short. You didn't say much. Could you come up with an imaginary man and describe him? Make him sound big and tough like a football player or wrestler."

Dotty wasn't getting the message, "I want to end this scam. Starting a whole new concept about the man I met and want to marry would only prolong it. I'm going to ignore him and just hope he goes away."

Dotty just shook her head, "Yeah, look how well that's worked for you so far. This crazy scam has been going on for months now."

The next night a text message alert sounded on Missy's phone.

###

ROD Hi Julie - How are you? How have you been doing? How is the virus cases over there?

###

Missy ignored the text message just as she told Dotty she would. Her head was starting to hurt trying to think of another angle to end the scam. Two days later another text message came. Missy was hiking on the trail with Puffy. She wanted this over so bad she stopped and sent a text message back. This turned out to be a bad idea. Rod kept the text messages coming one right after another as she hiked.

ROD   Hi Julie - How are you?

ME   I'm hiking.

ROD   OK dear are you done hiking? OK what are your plans for the rest of the day.

ME   Hiking - Eat dinner and call friends.

ROD   I really miss you here but am happy we are back together again. what really happened can you share with me? What really happened to the man you told me you are happy with?

ME   You were MIA for over a month. I'm dating a man here and it is serious.

ROD   Is okay I wish you well but we can be friends right.

ME   Yes, but don't ask favors.

ROD   Have you guys been able to meet or still chatting as we do here? Is okay I wish you well but we can be friends right. Why we make friends is to be of help and support when we need them Is a 50 50 something. Really that my favor is unreasonable. Well I understand cuz its not your problem and you are not in my shoes. Ever since the virus crisis started we have not been supply crds her in the Gorilla Camp Iraq you can go and make your research cuz what that clerk told is just ringing all over your head, what is my gain if I lie to you. You don't know what we are battling and passing through here. Me Will not send you anything. Am not asking for it. Just want to prove you wrong. Life is not just sitting from one side and judge or criticize others. I was thinking by you age you have seen and experiences things that you also have to see things in different dimensions before taking a final decision. The worst thing you could do now is stop talking to me as you have always do but I must tell you the truth.

ME   I will only believe you when we meet in person. Stop texting till then.

ROD   I'm not asking you for money all I need is a card to keep myself company as I can't get it here. Why are finding it difficult to understand that fact that is only someone in the state can get this card

ME   Bullshit if you are in the army you can get anything you want.

ROD   Really how did you come to conclusion and who told you that

ME   Because the army told me so.

ROD   Lol and you think I will be foolish to have something to do with you when am out from this jungle when you couldn't help and only doubted me.

Chapter 15

Those last text messages while she was hiking again scared her. She kept looking through every bush and checking the trail behind her. Never had she been so unnerved by something. The rapid text messages were beginning to blur. She was having trouble remembering what she last sent.

He had gone from sending romantic messages to threatening ones. Why would he go to this much trouble? It had to be clear to him she wasn't going to send him the card, so why did he ask for it again? At least the last text message sounded like he was finally going away. Was it really over?

Weeks went by without an email or text message from Rod. Missy decided to cancel the gmail account she had been using. She kept the same phone number on her cell since changing it would be a real hassle. It would be easy to just delete any text messages that came from him.

She would never again click on anything that she wasn't one hundred percent sure of. Missy had learned her lesson the hard way.

At least she didn't feel in danger anymore. Some other poor lonely little old ladies would probably end up with him.

There was still one thing that bothered her. The soldier in the photo was still on her phone. From time to time as she deleted messages from her friends, she would scroll to the bottom and there would be his photo. For some unknown reason she couldn't bring herself to delete it. It troubled her that he still didn't know what had happened with a scammer using his identity for such a prolonged scam.

What would he think about the crap this guy sent over the web while impersonating him. If it was her identity, she would definitely want to know about it. Missy knew this happened all the time from the email the army sent to her. That was a dead end since they would not assist her with notifying the soldier.

Missy began to feel like her life was back to normal and she worked on her next novel. She was still bored and was happy when Dotty called to ask if she would go with her to shop for new bedside lamps. She and Missy hopped into her car and drove to Silverdale where the shopping center was located.

Just like most things with Dotty, shopping was an exhausting venture. She went to store after store and checked out all the options. On the way to hopefully the last store, Missy spotted an army recruiting office. Without letting Dotty know her plan, she made an excuse to leave the store while Dotty shopped. Missy walked across the street and entered the office. She had no idea what to say.

"Hi, I know this is a long shot, but I have to try."

The officer gave her a curious look and asked, "What can I do for you?"

Missy decided to talk so fast, he wouldn't be able to interrupt her. "You're going to think I'm nuts, but I assure you my intentions are sincere. It's a long and involved story, so I'll try to be brief. I have spent the last few months corresponding with a scammer using the identity of an army soldier.

I knew from the beginning he was a scammer and I never sent him anything he wanted, especially money; but I felt bad for the soldier who had no idea his identity was being used this way. I had hoped to get some information that would lead to the identity of the scammer so he could be stopped, but that never happened.

At one point I notified the army about this but got an email back saying this sort of thing goes on all the time and to discontinue communication. They were not of any assistance in notifying the soldier involved. I have ended the scam, but still feel bad for the soldier. My only interest is in letting him know what happened. I have a photo of him with his name on his uniform - Stoddard. Can I give you this photo and the other information I have so you can notify him?"

Missy caught her breath, handed the photo and information to the officer, and realized she had said a lot. Did this guy understand what she wanted? Or would he just humor this silly lady?

His reply was the same as the one from the army email. "Ma'am, I know these types of scams go on, but there is little we can do about it. I'm glad you didn't comply with the scammer and ended it. We are not allowed to give out any information about army soldiers."

Missy wasn't going to be deterred. She hoped he had been listening to her elaborate tale and continued trying to persuade him.

"I realize that I don't want his information, just to have him notified what happened with his identity. There must be a way you can notify him or his family. That's all I want."

Missy could again see this was another dead end. The recruiter didn't look like he was taking her seriously.

He abruptly ended their conversation. "I'm sorry to not be of assistance to you but thank you for your interest."

Missy turned, walked out the door and across the street where Dotty was still shopping. She was so involved with finding a really nice pair of lamps, she didn't even ask where Missy had gone. Missy was so disappointed with her effort to notify the soldier, she never said anything to Dotty. It was a sad end to the scam episode. Rod had happily disappeared, but so had the hope of notifying the soldier. Still the thoughts about the soldier and his photo remained with Missy.

Chapter 16

The trepidation of opening her computer and seeing an email from Rod had disappeared for Missy. Several months had gone by without any text messages or emails, and now she was hard at work on her novel. The first novel was finished, and she was enthralled with the characters of the second novel. It was an easy escape from the reality of life under the depression of the pandemic.

Instead of talking to and seeing her friends, she was making new ones on the computer through the characters in her novel. Just like Dotty lived vicariously through her, Missy was living vicariously through the characters. They almost seemed real as she created them, just like the soldier in the photo on her phone that was still there.

The only text messages she received now were about setting tee times with her friends. At least she could spend some time outdoors with people not wearing masks. No one seemed concerned about the virus when playing golf outdoors on the wide-open fairways.

Missy was still happy with her life. Hiking on the trails with her dog, riding at the stable periodically, and playing golf filled her days.

Every morning was started on the computer with the new friends in her novel. The characters still seemed real as she chartered their lives for them in words.

As the pages were printed, she copied them, and gave Dotty a preview of the novel. This was the highlight of Dotty's day, since she was just as invested in the lives of Missy's characters. It was such a relief to read about this story instead of the emails and text messages that had been given to her during Missy's escapade with the scammer.

Missy's mind was spinning so fast with the words she wanted to put into the computer about her favorite character, she almost missed the text beep from her cell phone. That sound no longer brought the combination of fear, anxiety, and excitement she used to have during the scam. Now it was a pleasant tone that meant someone wanted to play golf. Susan had made a tee time for eleven AM the next day.

As she scrolled past the new text message she realized there was an overload of messages. It was a pain in the butt to delete each of them one at a time on the dumb phone, but she needed to do it. When she was almost finished, Missy saw the next one that she had saved for so long. It was a photo of the soldier. His smile seemed so real and friendly. What a nice man he must be. She should delete it too. Somehow she couldn't push the button and closed the phone. What she needed now was another cup of coffee before continuing with her novel, so she walked to the kitchen.

"Don't be so silly." she said to herself but knew she probably would never delete the photo. Her fantasy with the characters of her novel was bad enough. At least these people were not real and could never be hurt by anything more than the written situations she put them in. Somehow, she was always able to miraculously rescue them. Both of her novels would have happy endings just like she hoped for her life.

PART SECOND

Chapter 17

Missy put the thoughts of the soldier on her phone away and started writing about the newest character in her second novel. He was of course a handsome, well built, and charming man. Typical of most mystery novels.

Lost in her thoughts, Missy almost missed the sound that seldom came these days. It was the cowbell she hung up since her house didn't have a built-in doorbell. No one came to her house anymore since the Governor gave out the 'stay at home' order. The cowbell had been silent for a long time and the sound didn't register at first.

Missy finally woke up and walked to the door wondering who on earth could it be. She opened the door and in shock almost screamed, "Oh my God, you're real!"

Standing in the doorway was a soldier with the name on his uniform - STODDARD.

With a bit of a laugh Raine Stoddard replied, "Yeah, I'm pretty much real. People usually open their door and say hello."

Missy closed her gaping mouth and muttered, "You're the soldier in the photo from the scammer. I never thought you would ever be contacted, let alone have you standing at my door. Have you been told about the scammer and what I did? Somehow, you must have been. I can't believe you're here. How did you find me?"

"That was some speech and a lot of questions." Raine was silent for a moment. "Give me a minute to sort through this." He decided to give a short explanation of why he was at Missy's doorstep.

"That recruiter you went to have a change of heart after talking with you. He sent me the information you gave him. The army has a lot of resources available to locate people. Phone numbers and emails can be traced if you have access to the government web sites. You left a few breadcrumbs here and there and I put them together.

To tell you the truth, I'm just as surprised to be here. For whatever reason, your efforts to notify me of the scam stayed with me, and I just couldn't leave it alone. Sending a text message or email seemed wrong and even a card wasn't enough. I had to thank you in person, so here I am ringing your cowbell. Clever idea by the way.

I tried to call letting you know I was in town, but I got a voicemail. I was afraid a voicemail message or text would freak you out after what happened with the scam."

It was then Missy remembered her phone was in the kitchen and she wouldn't have heard it ring. Here he was, the soldier in the photo on her phone she had just looked at. His smile was even more inviting in person than the smile from the photo.

Missy was so stunned; she almost forgot her manners. They had been standing in the doorway for quite some time. Puffy, her dog, had forgotten her manners too, and was jumping up on the soldier's uniform to be petted.

"I'm so sorry, my dog is extremely friendly and loves everyone." Scolding the dog, Missy said, "Puffy, get down and leave the man alone."

Raine reached down and petted the dog, "I don't mind. I love dogs and Puffy is really cute and soft. I can see why you named her that, it is a she isn't it? Puffy would be an embarrassing name for a boy dog."

Missy smiled and admitted, "You're right, Puffy is a she and got her name because of her shaggy coat."

They stood in the doorway in an awkward silence for a moment. Missy was so astonished, she was speechless.

Raine started the conversation by wondering, "I'm surprised you were able to recognize me. It's been several months since you contacted the recruitment office and all you had was that photo."

Missy's smile changed to a shy grin and confessed, "This morning I got a text message from a friend and noticed there were way too many old text messages on my phone. I decided to delete them, but when I got to the bottom I couldn't delete the last one. Please come in, there's something I want to show you."

Missy went to the kitchen, got her phone, scrolled to messages, and opened the last text. It was the photo of the soldier sent by the scammer and held the phone to show Raine.

"This is the one I couldn't delete. It's the photo the scammer sent of the soldier he was impersonating -you."

The look on Raine's face said it all. This lady cared about him, even though all she had was a photo. He had no idea why, only that the recruitment agent said she had corresponded with the scammer for months. There must have been something personal going on for her to have kept the photo and been so determined to notify him.

Was it curiosity or an obligation for her efforts notifying him of the scam that was making him want to see her? Whatever it was, he was glad to be here, but what now? Again, there was an awkward moment as they both stood in the kitchen.

Missy, regaining her manners, asked, "Would you like to have some coffee or water or something?"

Thinking he wanted to get to know this lady who was so determined to be of assistance to him, Raine gladly accepted. "Yes, I think that would be nice. Coffee sounds great."

He was also curious about what had transpired between this lady and the scammer. According to the recruiter who notified him, the scam had gone on for several months.

Missy busied herself making coffee while Raine sat at the kitchen island. Not thinking he might be bringing up an unpleasant subject Raine asked, "Have you heard from the scammer lately?"

"No, thank goodness!" Missy replied emphatically.

Wanting to know why Missy tried so hard to notify him he asked, "What made you so determined to let me know about the scam? I'm also curious about why you kept the communication with the scammer going for so long. What type of messages did the scammer send to you?"

Missy felt slightly embarrassed to reveal everything about the scam, but this man was the main reason for continuing the scam. She felt he had a right to know the whole story.

Missy started at the beginning, "At first I thought he was a soldier, especially when I got the photo. The poor spelling, grammar, and request for an iTune card gave him away. I found out scammers request iTune cards because they can be converted, and the scammer can end up with cash.

After that I was angry he would use the identity of a soldier for his scam. It wouldn't have been so bad if he used an average Joe, but to use a soldier

who was risking his life to protect my country was too much. That really pissed me off. I hoped by keeping the scam going, I could get some piece of information to identify or locate him.

I kept this thing going for over three months. I know that was silly. He was probably in some third world country sitting in a cube with a dozen guys doing the same thing. I tried to trace the phone number he used. It was from a text only company in Carrollton, Texas near Dallas. His email was from Google and that was a dead end too."

Raine was amazed how tenacious this lady was and pleased she felt that strong about soldiers and asked, "Did you finally give up when you couldn't find him?"

Missy was hesitant to tell him how many times she had vacillated between stopping and continuing the scam.

"At first it was all about the iTune card and wanting a relationship. His emails were so sappy and ridiculous my friend, Dotty and I laughed."

Finally, he started asking for my phone number and address to send me some money he confiscated. I tried to put him off for a while, but eventually he said someone would come to my house and deliver the money.

That was when I really got scared and ended it. We had several nasty text messages at the end that was almost like a boyfriend and girlfriend breakup. It was really creepy. Fortunately, the scam finally ended."

Raine was puzzled, "That sounds like an extreme scam. You told the recruiter you never sent him anything. I'd think the typical scammer would move on. Why would he continue for so long if he wasn't getting what he asked for?"

Missy didn't have an answer for Raine's question, "I don't know, I've never done anything like that before and never will again. It was probably a foolish thing to do."

A little embarrassed Missy admitted, "I did spend way too much time on my computer with that scammer guy. Dotty and I got caught up with the game we were playing with the scammer. I guess we were bored from isolation due to the pandemic. We were also intrigued with the constant, crazy, and weird text messages and emails he sent.

He told me some stuff that he made up about you, but of course that wasn't true. We're sort of in the same boat you and me. I'd like to get to know you. You're in uniform. Are you still in the army? Sorry, that's all wrong. The scammer guy said you were going to retire soon, and I guess that was still in my mind."

It dawned on Raine that Missy likely had a lot of misinformation about him from the scammer that was probably confusing.

"I don't know what the scammer said about me. Maybe it would be better if we start as if the scam never happened and we just met the normal way. I have retired as of last week. If I stay in uniform I can fly free on a military transport. I just haven't changed clothes today. I flew into the Naval Air Force Base on Whidbey Island this morning and rented a car. I took the ferry across and decided to come see you before it got too late in the evening."

The coffee finished perking, Missy poured two cups, and passed one to Raine. To move on from the scam conversation Missy asked, "Do you take anything in your coffee?"

"Yes, milk or cream if you have it."

Missy offered, "I have milk or this creamer if you like it."

Raine slid his coffee mug across to Missy, "Whatever you're using is fine with me."

Suddenly it occurred to Missy she didn't know this man's first name, just his last name printed on his uniform. "I guess we haven't been formally introduced. My name is Missy Wilhelm."

"Raine Stoddard and I'm really glad we've met, even though it is a bit unconventional. I noticed your goats when I drove up. They ran to the fence to greet me just like Puffy."

Raine thought - 'that was a dumb thing to say'. He was at a bit of a loss as to what to say to Missy that didn't make him sound like a schoolboy who just discovered he liked a girl.

He usually didn't have that problem, but there was something about this lady. Maybe it was the fact she was interested enough in him to keep his photo.

Wanting to know more about Missy, Raine asked, "What do you usually do with your day besides conversations with scammers on your computer? I'm sorry, that was a rude question, please forgive me. I just want to get to know you. I'm sure you have interests other than corresponding with scammers." Raine was now definitely at a loss for words.

Thankfully Missy continued the conversation. "I write mystery novels on my computer now, and was working on another one when you rang my cowbell. That's what I do with most of my morning and sometimes in the early evening, like today.

In the afternoon I take Puffy on hikes over at the spit trail and spend time with the goats while they do their mowing and weed-eating job. Some afternoons I play golf with my friends.

132

That seemed logical to Raine, "So writing emails to the scammer was probably easy for you. Sorry, we need to keep off that subject." Raine chastised himself again for saying something rude. "You said another novel, so you're an author. Have you published some novels?"

"No, this is the second one and it's not something I thought I would ever do. It just came to me, and I couldn't stop. I don't know anything about publishing a novel and haven't looked into the process."

Missy didn't want to get into the reason for starting the first book, so she changed the subject. "Where are you originally from?"

Raine had been puzzled by something Missy said, "That's the strange thing. You said the scammer info was from Carrollton near Dallas. I'm from Weatherford near Fort Worth, not far from Dallas. Sorry, I know we wanted to get off that subject, but it seems strange."

Missy felt goose bumps on her arms. "The scammer said 'you' were from Dallas. You lived there with your daughter and that you had been married. He also mentioned you were an engineer. Do you think it wasn't a coincidence that he picked you?"

"Now you are scaring me," Raine said, thinking that was too strange. "I don't think a scammer could have gotten my personal information. No, that would be a one in a million chance. Besides, when I was in high school my Dad and I moved to Connecticut. After I graduated, I joined the army to get an education.

We didn't have any money for college and prospects for jobs that paid anything were nonexistent. The army was my best option and it turned out to be a good fit. I was able to get an engineering degree. I can't imagine the scammer saying he was an engineer had anything to do with me. My work for the army as an engineer has never been made public."

Missy thought she should put the coincidences in the information from the scammer about Raine to rest.

"One thing I concluded about the scammer was that he wasn't very sophisticated and didn't have technical skills available to him. Surely, he wouldn't have been able to get your personal information. I do wonder how he got your photo."

Raine had the answer, "It was used for recruitment advertising a few years ago."

Finally, the subject of the scammer changed to both Missy and Raine exchanging small details about their lives and some common interests.

Chapter 18

The conversation between Missy and Raine was effortless and rambled on for a couple hours. Missy's stomach started growling and she realized dinner hadn't started.

"Would you like to stay for dinner? I'm not a great cook, but I can whip up something for us."

It occurred to Raine he had been talking to Missy much longer than his intention. His plan was to just stop by and say thanks. He hadn't intended to stay for coffee, but there was something very inviting about Missy that had drawn him in.

"That's okay, I don't want to intrude on the rest of your day."

Missy was about to blush at the thought of spending a meal with this handsome man and knew Dotty would think she was way too forward with a stranger. Somehow he didn't seem like a stranger. Maybe it was the numerous times she had looked at his photo, or the ease of their conversation.

"I'd be glad to have you stay," Missy added, "Besides with this crazy pandemic, it's difficult to get something to eat in town with the restaurants closed. I can fix a simple dinner for two. It's not a problem and we can get to know each other better."

Missy quickly thought to herself, what was she saying? Why would this man want to get to know her? She was a silly lady who conversed with a scammer for over three months while looking at a photo of him.

Raine had been traveling for several days and his meals had been sporadic. Missy was right, the only option he had seen for a meal was fast food and he was tired of that. A home cooked meal sounded so good. Besides, he was really starting to like Missy.

"I'd like to stay. Is there anything I can do to help?"

Missy decided on a quick and easy meal and told Raine, "Not really, tell me more about yourself. Do you have relatives in the area?"

"No, I just have my dad and he still lives in Connecticut. I was an only child and so was my dad, our family tree is pretty much a bush. And no, I've never been married or have a daughter like the scammer told you."

Missy was relieved to hear that. The marriage and daughter part of the soldier's description by the scammer was made up and didn't relate to Raine. To get back to a normal conversation, Missy asked, "Have you been to the Pacific Northwest before?"

"No, I've never been west of Texas." Raine continued with a brief description of his service. "The greatest part of my career has been overseas. I spent a lot of time in Germany. I've done several tours in Iraq.

For the most part I've been stationed on the East Coast. That worked out great since I could spend time with my dad. It's just been the two of us and my grandparents since I was in diapers."

Missy began to see a bit of sadness on Raine's face with that last sentence. She didn't think it appropriate to ask and started to serve the toasted tuna and cheese sandwiches and tomato soup she made. She handed two plates and bowls to Raine and suggested he set the table. They sat, ate the sandwiches and soup with Puffy as an audience. A bit of crust was offered to the ever so patient dog who would be next to receive her dinner.

With dinner finished and the dishes done, they sat on the couch with a glass of wine and talked for a while. Raine was interested in the stories Missy was writing and how she developed the plots. As Raine talked about the countries where he served, it appeared to Missy he was fading and tired.

She asked, "Would you like to sit for a minute while I feed the goats. Then I'll make some coffee. Those goats are quite comical when they think I'm

going to feed them. You can watch from the couch."

When Missy returned to the house, Raine had laid back on the couch and fallen asleep. He looked so comfy; Missy decided to let him sleep. She didn't know if he had already checked into a motel or had a place to stay, but they could figure that out when he woke up.

Missy started working on her novel and got totally involved as usual.

Noticing it was dark and 9:30, she looked over at Raine who was still sleeping. Missy could hardly believe the soldier she had coveted for so long was actually here. He was just as handsome asleep as awake. She stood for a moment watching him slowly and softly breathe.

She didn't have the heart to wake and ask him to leave, so she tossed a throw over him and let this stranger sleep on the couch for the night. Now Dotty would definitely have something to say about this. Missy could already hear her voice shouting, "The thing with the scammer was crazy enough, but letting a perfectly strange man sleep on your couch is way over the top."

Missy was scared by the scammer but felt completely safe with Raine sleeping on the couch. Besides, she could put a chair under her bedroom door

handle like they do in the movies. This thought made her laugh. Why was she so happy to have this man in her house? Yeah, he was the man she had looked at in the photo and coveted for months. Not only was he real, but he was also here and sleeping on her couch.

Her next thought was, get a hold of yourself girl. He will leave in the morning and you'll never see him again. He was very polite and came to see her in person. Missy supposed since he had retired, wasting time coming to see her wasn't a big thing. He probably had plans that would take him away, especially since he said his dad lived in Connecticut.

At least it's a happy ending to the story of the scammer. Just meeting Raine made the entire time she spent with the scammer worth it. Wouldn't it be a shock to the scammer to know he actually did her a favor and brought a handsome, nice, and real man into her life.

Chapter 19

When Missy woke up she went to her bedroom door and opened it just a crack to peak out. She wanted to see if her soldier was still asleep on the couch. The opening was just wide enough for Puffy to squeeze through. She ran to the couch but was a little bit suspicious of someone lying there and gently put her paws on the edge and sniffed Raine's arm. He woke up seeing Puffy and Missy looking at him.

Missy smiled, saying, "Good morning sleepyhead." Puffy took that as her cue and jumped on the couch and snuggled next to Raine.

Missy admonished the dog, "Puffy leave the man alone."

Quite embarrassed Raine admitted, "It's okay, I'm so sorry. I can't believe I slept here all night. I closed my eyes for a minute, and I was out."

Missy was secretly pleased he had. "You looked so peaceful; I didn't want to wake you. I figured if you fell asleep that easily, you must be very tired, so I just let you sleep as long as you needed."

Raine sat up still apologizing, "I haven't slept much lately. Transports are noisy and uncomfortable unlike your couch which felt great. The lack of sleep, good food, and wine did me in. Again, I'm sorry to have intruded and fallen asleep on your couch. I need to go into town to a motel and get cleaned up."

Being very forward Missy asked, "Where are you heading to next now that we've had our visit?"

"I haven't thought that far ahead. I suppose I'll go back to Port Townsend today and take the ferry to Whidbey. I can wait there for a flight."

There was a hesitation in Raine's voice that hinted he didn't have a definite plan for a destination. It was just enough to encourage Missy.

Wanting to spend more time with Raine and being quite bold Missy offered, "You're welcome to use the guest bath if you like. It's silly to rent a motel room for a shower. Just check the shampoo bottles. Some of them are for Puffy."

Raine already felt embarrassed enough as it was. "I've put you out too much as it is. I can get a room and some breakfast in town."

Not one to give up easily Missy pushed on. She had wanted to know him for so long and wasn't ready for this man to leave. Trying not to sound too anxious she said, "The only breakfast you'll get in town is an egg type muffin at a fast-food place. I'm not much of a cook, but I make a great breakfast. Bacon and eggs, french toast, blueberry and pecan pancakes. Whatever you like. Besides, I'd like the company. Puffy isn't much of a conversationalist."

Raine couldn't help toying between thinking he shouldn't stay and wanting to. At the last minute he admitted, "You had me at blueberry and pecan pancakes. I have a sweet tooth and I'm hungry."

As much as he felt slightly uncomfortable at spending so much time at a stranger's house, there was something about Missy that made him feel welcome.

"Thanks for your hospitality, I'll be glad to get out of this uniform. There are civilian clothes in my car. There is just one thing I'd like to know. I hope you're not going to make a habit of letting guys who ring the cowbell in to sleep on your couch."

Missy had to laugh and teased him, "You're the only one so far."

With concern Raine asked, "So far?"

"Well, I don't know how many handsome and sexy guys are out there wanting to ring my cowbell."

Raine asked, "Do they have to be handsome and sexy to qualify?"

"Yeah, pretty much," was Missy's sassy answer.

Blushing at the idea, Missy thought he was handsome and sexy, "In that case I'm honored."

Missy again teased him, "You do realize I recognized you from the photo a scammer sent me. Considering that, it's a good thing you're nice enough looking to qualify for ringing my cowbell."

Not wanting to dismiss his intention, Raine added, "Really, I'm serious about this. I know you were only playing a game with the scammer, but you took that game too far and it scared you."

Seeing the thoughtful look on Raine's face she said, "Don't worry, the only guy I'm letting sleep on my couch has to have the name Stoddard on his uniform."

Missy was trying hard not to beam with a huge grin that was begging to appear on her face. "I'll put on some coffee. Then I'm getting dressed and going out to feed the goats, so take your time."

Breakfast was started by the time Raine emerged from the bathroom. As handsome as he looked in his uniform, Raine was even more sexy in jeans and a tee shirt. Whatever he did in the military kept him lean and fit. To keep her mind from wandering where it shouldn't go, Missy kept him busy making another pot of coffee and setting the table. She also gave him the recipe for Puffy's breakfast and let him feed the dog.

During their meal once again, conversation was easy. Missy still wanted to know, "What are your plans now that you have found me?" Thinking that question could be misconstrued, she quickly added, "I don't mean for me, just in general now that you're retired."

Raine had to laugh because he was thinking about what he wanted to do since he was attracted to Missy. He wanted to say that he would like to get to know her better but thought it best to stick to the subject she was asking.

"I've had a lot of ideas, but nothing has really sounded right. I have an engineering degree that I could use, but I just left a full-time career and don't really want another. I'm not even sure where I want to live. My dad is in Connecticut, and it would be nice to be close to him, but I hate the East Coast. Way too many storms and it's either hot or cold. I've been stationed all over the east and there isn't any part of it I liked.

There are some places I've ruled out - California for one. Way too many people. I also don't like big cities. I've never been in the Pacific Northwest before. There seem to be a lot of small towns here on the Peninsula."

Raine suddenly came up with an idea that would give him an opportunity to spend time with Missy. "Maybe you could show me around."

Missy was in need of squashing a grin once more, "I could be your tour guide. That would be fun." Missy's next thought was 'whoa dummy, don't act like a schoolgirl and get ahead of yourself.'

Raine got up from the table and picked up his plate. Now he had a destination in mind. Right here with Missy, who seemed to be as attracted to him as he was to her.

"Let me help you with the dishes and then I'll go to town. If we are going to explore this area, I'll need to get a motel room. Not that your couch wasn't nice, but I'm afraid Puffy would abandon you for my lap and that just wouldn't do. We can start our tour today, that is if you're free this afternoon."

Not to sound too eager, even though she was, Missy suggested, "I have a few things to do and then I can meet you in town."

After they finished the dishes and another cup of coffee, Raine started for the door and said, "I'll text you the name of the motel and room number when I get there."

The minute Raine was out the door Missy grabbed her phone. She was going nuts waiting to tell Dotty all about Raine. She couldn't call her with Raine in the house since it would be impolite to make a call, especially with what she wanted to say.

Dotty was not a morning person and didn't like calls before 9 AM, so this after breakfast call was perfect. Missy made the call she had dreamed of making, "Dotty, I have something incredibly amazing to tell you, I'm coming over."

Dotty could only think - 'what is she up to now', "Considering some of the stuff you come up with, I probably need to cancel coffee and have a stiff drink ready."

Driving to Dotty's house Missy almost broke the land speed record. Dotty opened the door and Missy quickly stepped in with eager anticipation.

Missy took a quick breath and began, "You may need two stiff drinks. I hope you're ready for this. I know I wasn't, but I'm over the moon now. Yesterday my cowbell on the front porch rang and you will never believe who was standing there. It was the soldier from the photo."

Shocked, Dotty shouted, "Oh my God, the scammer?"

"No, Raine Stoddard, the real soldier in uniform and all."

Dotty sat down and was in need of that stiff drink. After a long gulp she questioned, "You're putting me on."

"No, he is here. Well not right now, he went to town to check into a motel. He wanted to thank me in person for notifying him about the scam, so he came to my house. I invited him in for coffee and we talked for a long time."

Scolding, Dotty told her, "Of course you did. A strange man you know nothing about, and you let him in your house. Missy, didn't you learn anything from your experience with the scammer?"

"Dotty, he's not a scammer. He's the soldier in the photo and he looks even better in person. You should see him in jeans and a tee shirt. He's really sexy."

Missy suddenly knew she goofed since she said he showed up in his uniform, but Dotty didn't seem to catch it. To cover her mistake Missy admitted, "If I haven't shocked you enough there's more."

Dotty walked to the kitchen for a refill, "I'm afraid to ask, will I need another drink first?"

Giggling Missy added, "You might, he stayed for dinner."

Knowing her culinary skills Dotty wondered, "Missy, you don't cook. What could you feed him?"

"I'm not totally without cooking skills." Missy defended herself, "I made toasted tuna and cheese sandwiches with tomato soup. He liked it. For the next thing that happened I'm going to suggest you make that drink a double."

Returning with a drink Dotty said, "Lay it on me."

"Funny you should say it like that. We sat on the couch for a while talking after dinner and having wine. Then I went down to feed the goats. While I was gone he fell asleep lying on the couch. He looked so cute and sweet I just couldn't wake him. So, I tossed a throw over him, and he slept there all night."

Missy covered her ears knowing what was to come.

Dotty was now screaming, "You have to be out of your mind! It was bad enough inviting him into your house in the first place but having him sleep in your house! Next you're going to tell me he took a shower too."

Missy was silent. There were no words that could explain what she knew was probably crazy. She was ready for one of the best scolding yet from Dotty.

"No way. I'm going to have you locked up in the booby hatch. You need to be protected from yourself. One of these days I'm going to see the story of how you were murdered on Dateline.

I've never met anyone who could make the dumbest choices you do. After what went on with the scammer, why would you do something that foolish with a man you just met. You're going to give me a heart attack if you don't get some common sense."

Missy was right, that was one of Dotty's best reprimands yet. The only problem was what she said was true. There must be an angel looking over her considering some of her choices concerning men these days. Somehow Raine felt like a smart choice.

What Dotty said left Missy confused about her feelings.

She had been looking at the photo of Raine on her phone for months. Had all the romantic stuff from the scammer affected how she felt about the man in the photo? Does that have something to do with seeing him now or was she attracted to Raine in the normal way? Regardless, she was definitely attracted to him.

She had to get the memory of the scammer out of her mind. The man who came to her house was real. Even though he was connected to the scammer in a way, this was the start of something new and she was eager to see where it would lead.

Chapter 20

Making plans for her new tour guide job with Raine was easy. Missy had lots of great ideas that could encompass several days if he was up for it. She arrived at the Holiday Inn and knocked on room 102. The smile on Raine's face when he opened the door was all Missy needed to confirm all her tour guide ideas.

Their first trek would be the trail at the spit where she walked Puffy every day. Puffy had to stay home because dogs were not allowed on the trail to the beach. Missy usually skipped this trail when walking Puffy. She volunteered to drive to the Dungeness Wildlife Refuge Park so Raine could sight-see. They walked along the bluff trail and stopped at one of the lookouts on the edge overlooking the ocean.

Missy started with her guide narration, "This is the Strait of Juan de Fuca and across there is Vancouver Island and the city of Victoria, BC. The other pieces of land you can see are San Juan and Lopez Islands."

Raine was taking it all in and asked, "Where is Whidbey Island?"

"It's farther to the east."

Raine remembered something from the night on Missy's couch, "Last night I woke up for a minute and thought I was dreaming when I heard the sound of waves breaking. I didn't realize your house was so close to the ocean."

"I heard the waves break a few times last night too," recalled Missy. "I like the sound. It's peaceful. Sometimes the fog banks come in and I can hear the foghorn. Add that to the sound of the waves crashing and it's like ocean music."

A visual picture came to Raine that encompassed the fog and waves and the sounds. He stood for a moment taking it in. It was like his world had opened up looking across part of the Pacific ocean to Canada. He felt relaxed and free, but mostly happy. Any plans he needed for the future could wait.

Missy took the trail to the beach and spit leading to the New Dungeness lighthouse. Raine stopped and looked down the spit to the lighthouse. "How far is it to the lighthouse?"

"About five miles out and five miles back. It's quite a trek and it's best to do it at low tide. I went out there with some friends last summer for a tour. We cheated and took a boat ride. The lighthouse can be rented, and the guests are docents, or at least it used to be before the virus caused it to be closed."

A bit disappointed, Raine commented, "Too bad. It looks interesting, but you're right it's a long way to hike."

Resuming the trail, they entered the forest thick with fir, cedar, maple trees, sallow bushes, and ferns. The forest trail opened to a view of the valley below. A bench sat on the edge. Raine asked Missy to sit with him while he looked out over the farmland fields.

Raine looked out at the valley below with a wistful expression, "I like all the farmland around this area. It reminds me of where I grew up in Texas."

Missy wanted to know more about this man and asked, "What was your childhood like in Texas?"

"It was just my dad and grandparents. We all lived in a small house just outside of town. I played the usual sports in school and got okay grades. My life was fairly normal until high school when my dad and I moved to Connecticut. My uncle got sick and needed help with his construction business."

Missy asked about his name, "Is Raine a nickname? It's unusual."

"No, it's my given name. My mother's name was Storm. I guess she had a sense of humor."

Missy was now even more curious about him, forgot her manners, and started asking quite personal questions. "What was she like to have such a different name?"

Evidently Raine didn't think anything of it and answered, "I think she earned it. I don't know very much. My dad wouldn't talk about her. She died at eighteen just a few months after I was born.

My grandmother told me she was a party girl. I got the impression she didn't approve of her. She said my dad only married her because she got pregnant and had to drop out of high school. For some reason everyone seemed to avoid the subject."

Continuing with her personal questions Missy asked, "May I ask what happened to her?"

"All I know is she lost control of her car and it went into a ravine," explained Raine. "No one would say how it happened. I like to think it was an accident, but who knows."

Missy admonished herself for the questions she asked. There wasn't any way she could have known his background was troubled. She was beginning to see how different she and Raine were. He probably didn't have the wonderful childhood she did.

Would that difference in their childhoods be a problem now that they were adults? A lot can change from childhood to becoming an adult. Maybe the difference didn't matter. She had to become stronger because of the sheltered life she started out with. Maybe he had to become stronger because of his difficult childhood and it appeared he had. The stripes and bars on his uniform proved it.

She was also surprised at herself for asking the questions. Dotty was the one who always talked a blue streak with people and came away with their entire life story. Even more surprising was that he so easily revealed what was probably a challenging childhood.

Missy was pleased he wanted to spend time with her, and she could learn something about him. Now the photo on her phone she looked at so many times was a real person. A person she was becoming fond of.

Raine surprised himself by talking so much. It was easy with Missy. She listened and seemed genuinely interested. It occurred to him he hadn't thought about his mother since he enlisted just after high school. The past wasn't something he wanted to revisit. Even talking about his dad brought back one of the last conversations he and his dad exchanged.

Those thoughts were starting to darken his mood and he would put them out of his mind. He wanted to change the subject and asked Missy about her childhood. "How about your childhood?"

Since Raine told her about his childhood, Missy began about hers, "My parents owned and operated a hotel in Portland, Oregon. I was a city girl who longed to be a country girl. My education came from the variety of guests at the hotel. I met people from all over the world.

It was an old-fashioned hotel in downtown, sort of iconic. It had been in the family for decades. From the time I was a little girl, I worked along with my parents to operate the hotel. When my parents passed, it wasn't the same, so I sold the hotel and moved away from the city. I married and finally got to live in the country just as I had always dreamed. We had a farm with a variety of animals and grew farm to table organic vegetables. In short I married, didn't have children, divorced, and eventually moved here."

Missy mentioned an ex-husband and Raine decided to ask, "What became of the ex-husband?"

Not really wanting to elaborate on her ex, Missy gave a short answer, "He began to self-destruct with alcohol, and I didn't want to be around at the end. I haven't seen or heard from him for a dozen years. I suppose he's still on the farm growing vegetables and drinking."

They resumed their hike on the trail along the forest and back to Missy's car. The day was getting late and Missy remembered, "I don't know about you, but it's been a long time since lunch and I'm getting hungry. We should start to think about dinner."

Raine was hungry too. He bought a burger before Missy picked him up, but it was long gone. "I'd like to take you out to dinner, but I don't know how to do that with the restaurants closed."

Missy was pleased and knew just what to say, "You said it, 'take out.' We can call a restaurant with an order, pick it up, and eat at my house. Does that sound good to you?"

"Okay, you decide which one to call since you're familiar with the restaurants. I'm open to any type of food." Raine was pleased with the suggestion. He really didn't have a plan for dinner and Missy was right about the restaurants. As they drove through town most of them appeared to be closed.

Missy had an idea. "There's a Mexican restaurant I'm fond of owned by a nice family. We can look up their menu online and order whatever you like. I have tequila and mix for margaritas at home too."

Raine was pleased he would be spending another meal with Missy. "That sounds great to me."

With their selections made from the menu, their order phoned in, Raine and Missy arrived at the restaurant. Raine was pleased to see there was actually a family working together preparing meals. He approached the register to pay for the meals and spoke Spanish to the owner. They had a short conversation Missy couldn't follow since she didn't speak Spanish. Naturally, Raine being from Texas where there is a large Mexican population might be able to speak Spanish.

It pleased her that he would be polite and friendly with the owner and wanted to let him know.

"That was quite nice of you to speak to the owner in Spanish. What did you say?"

"I thanked him for making an effort to stay open and provide a meal for us to enjoy. He said they're struggling but are determined to keep their restaurant. It's the future for their children. He thanked us for supporting them. I told him we would be back, and I hoped we could enjoy his restaurant when we could be seated inside."

Missy knew the type of people in town and said, "I doubt there are other people in this town who speak to him in Spanish. Thank you for that. I'm sure it meant a lot to him."

Raine knew how lucky he was to have a guaranteed income from his military retirement. He couldn't imagine how he would feel if he was a restaurant owner. "It was the least I could do besides ordering our dinner."

Chapter 21

When dinner was finished Raine had a question for Missy. "What's on our tour list for tomorrow if you're still up to being my guide? I know I'm taking a lot of your time, and you must have other things to do, but I'm enjoying spending time with you and getting to know this area."

How could Missy say anything negative to that? She was enjoying spending time with him.

"Being a tour guide for you is fun for me too. It's been a long time since I explored my own back yard. I enjoy seeing the interest and excitement in you.

You'll find out the nicest part of retirement is doing whatever you want whenever you want and that's just what I'm doing. Let's keep going. There's a lot yet to see. How about a tour of the port towns? We can start with Port Townsend."

Raine was so interested in the operation of the ferry crossing the sound, he didn't pay much attention to the town where it arrived. His concentration was on the car's Mapquest directing him to Sequim.

Chapter 22

Missy looked at her phone and noticed a couple missed calls from Dotty. She had been so caught up thinking about all the great places she could take Raine, she almost forgot about Dotty. Since Dotty was a night owl, a late evening call after returning from the grocer would be acceptable and very much appreciated.

"Dotty, I'm so sorry for not keeping you in the loop. The truth is I've been totally focused on Raine."

Dotty realized why she had been put on the back burner. This mysterious man was still around.

"Your soldier is still in town? What do you mean focused on him? What have you been doing since you let him sleep on your couch? Have you been spending time with him? He isn't still staying at your house is he?"

"Dotty, quit asking so many questions. I can't even remember them all. I'll start with the one you're most interested in. No, he is not staying at my house. He checked into a motel. Yes, I've been spending time with him. He wanted to see more of this area, so he asked if I would be his sort of tour guide. He's a very nice man and I'm perfectly safe with him if that's what's worrying you."

Missy's safety wasn't all Dotty was worried about. She thought all along Missy was too concerned about the soldier in the photo right from the beginning of the scam session. Was she transferring some of the stuff from the scammer onto this guy? And, did she have silly romantic notions from looking at that photo for all those months? Was that making her attracted to the real man? Missy was playing a mind game with the scammer. Had the game advanced to this man? Dotty wanted to be an advocate for Missy who was always too nice and a bit naive with people.

"Missy, what do you really know about this man? He shows up out of the blue on your doorstep. Falls asleep on your couch and the next thing you're a tour guide for him. Where have you been going?"

Since Dotty liked to play mother hen, Missy knew what she would be up against. "He's not a serial killer or a scam artist, Dotty. He's very polite, respectful, and so far has not given me any indication he wants anything more than my company and a tour of the area. Why are you so worried?"

Dotty was more than ready to give Missy her opinion, "How can you ask me to not worry after what you went through with the scammer. You are way too nice to people, and they are always taking advantage of you.

Maybe he's playing the long game. He will get you romantically involved, which you easily do, and then reveal his true intentions just like the scammer guy tried. It was bad enough with the scam because that was done with text messages and email. This is a live person you are alone with."

Missy was more than ready to defend Raine, "I may not be as skeptical of people as I should, but he seems to be quite genuine. He told me a lot about himself and opened up to me. So far we had a hike at the spit, got take-out Mexican for dinner, and today we went on a port town tour of Port Townsend, Fort Flagler, and Port Ludlow.

Tomorrow we're going to Carol and Chet's lake cabin to play with the water toys. I really like him Dotty, and I promise to be careful and not get carried away, although it won't be easy. He's quite handsome and I bet he's going to be very sexy in swim trunks."

Missy laughed thinking how much fun it is to shock Dotty. It was worth it even though she would get another earful.

"There you go again. I know this is a bad idea. You're going to get in trouble one way or another. Now I'm left here sitting around worrying about you. I've never known anyone who could get themselves into so many messes. It's like you somehow silently advertise - come and get me, I'm vulnerable. It's a good thing you have me to try to rein you in. Sorry about the pun."

Missy had to laugh again, "Dotty, you're my loyal friend and I know you have my best interests at heart. Just think how boring your life would be without all the shenanigans I come up with. I promise to let you keep me on the straight and narrow.

I'll take it slow with Raine and keep you informed if anything suspicious comes up. For now, I'm going to enjoy spending time with him and see where this goes. He's never been married and his only relative is his dad who lives in Connecticut.

He just retired from the Army and hasn't decided what to do next. So, he's free to do whatever he decides. I think he's just trying to find out who he is now that he's no longer a soldier. It's probably difficult.

I'm going to take this one day at a time and plan some fun stuff for us to do. Please don't worry about me. That escapade with the scammer did teach me something and I'll be careful. Right now, I'm tired and going to bed alone. Good night."

Chapter 23

———————————

The next morning Missy asked Raine to come for breakfast before starting their tour. She hated the idea of him having to start the day with fast food. They worked together putting the ingredients for an omelet in a saucepan. With the addition of toast breakfast was ready.

Raine still didn't know where they were going to spend the day. He asked, "You're still not telling me what we're doing or where we're going today?"

"No, it's a surprise," Missy answered with a mischievous look on her face. "Don't worry, you're going to have a great time and you'll need a good breakfast for the activities I have planned. We'll be gone all day, so I made us lunch to take along. By the way, you can swim can't you?"

"Yeah, I can swim. Now I'm really curious. Can you give me a clue?"

"I think you'll be happy with my surprise." Missy gave Raine her reason for the secret. "It's more fun for me that way."

Raine was pleased Missy was having fun but was concerned about taking up so much of her time.

Missy, I'm having a very good time with you as my tour guide and the places you're taking me. I feel guilty for taking up so much of your days. You must have other friends you spend time with. What about the other things you need to do?"

"Remember what I told you about retirement," Missy reminded Raine. "This is what I want to do. Don't worry, my social calendar isn't going to be overly interrupted. With this virus most of my friends are staying home and only communicating by phone or email.

Spending time with a live person is a treat. I haven't been able to have outings lately, so this is an opportunity for me too. Time's wasting, the dishes need to be cleaned and then let's get on the road."

The drive took them along the Hood Canal. They made a couple stops at scenic points. Raine took an interest in the oyster harvesting and was curious about geoducks.

Missy explained to him that she had a minuscule pallet when it came to seafood. "If you want to try some of these, you're on your own. I told you I don't cook, and oysters and geoducks are definitely way out of my expertise. Sorry, I'm not sure I would even want to watch you eat them."

Raine laughed, "Don't worry, my interest is only in learning about them, not consuming them. I'm a basic meat and potato type of guy."

After a couple of other stops to check out the beautiful scenes of the canal, Missy turned off the highway onto the road to the cabin. She parked and they walked up to the deck with a view of the lake.

Raine took in the scene and expressed, "Wow, I like your surprise. Is this why you asked if I could swim?"

"Let's go in the cabin and get into swimsuits. You can borrow one of Chet's swim trunks. He's about your size."

They started with the paddle boat for a trip across the lake and a view of the mountains. To cool off, they swam from the dock to the neighboring homes and back. After lunch they paddled the kayaks across the lake. Missy had to laugh at Raine. He was like a little boy who couldn't decide which water toy to play with first.

Missy watched as he put on the snorkel and mask to explore the lake bottom near the shore. When he finally got tired, they stretched out on the chaise lounges to relax in the warm sunshine.

Missy teasingly wanted to know, "Did you find any hidden treasure down there?"

"No, you're out of luck, just a bunch of beer bottles." Raine looked over at Missy and smiled, "This is the best day yet. You were right about keeping today a surprise. It's more fun this way. I can't tell you how nice it feels to lie here, listen to the waves splashing against the dock and relax.

You have some really nice friends to let us come here and enjoy the lake. When I was a kid one of my friends' parents took us to a lake, but it wasn't anything like this one. What a beautiful place this is. Thank you for bringing me here."

"You're welcome. I'm having fun watching the enjoyment you get from our trips. I have to admit I had an alternative reason for coming to the lake. I was anxious to see you wearing nothing more than swim trunks."

Raine laughed and put Missy on the spot, "What do you think?"

Missy blushed and reminded him, "I think you're a very handsome and sexy man. Just the type I let sleep on my couch after ringing the cowbell."

Thinking back to that night, Raine smiled, "Thanks and I have to say you looked mighty fine in your swimsuit. Is that a blush I see on your cheeks?"

Truly embarrassed, Missy denied her rosy cheeks, "No, it's a bit of sunburn. As much as I like lying here in the sun, we should pack up and head for home. Are you hungry again? We can finish the chicken salad."

Raine felt his stomach rumble, "Yeah, it can be an early dinner. I did work up an appetite snorkeling. I must say I hate to see our day end. Thanks again, you found the perfect outing. I haven't enjoyed a day this much for years. I'd like to thank Carol and Chet for letting us spend the day here."

That statement from Raine made Missy realize the only person who actually knew the story about Raine was Dotty. The request for the use of the cabin was sent by a text message, and only mentioned she would be with a friend. She was hesitant to get into a long explanation on the phone about Raine. Carol hadn't asked about the friend, just told her where the key was hidden, and she was welcome to use the cabin and water toys. Text messages, which she disliked, were handy if you didn't want to say much.

It was time to find out how Raine felt about meeting her friends. "Raine, I have several inquisitive friends who feel it's their right to keep track of my life. They're all going to be very curious about you. I'm not sure how to explain the way we met that would make sense.

My friends already know I'm capable of coming up with some unusual activities and ideas. I don't have any concerns about how we met, but it's a bit out of the norm even for me.

I'm afraid the story of our friendship would require a lengthy explanation. It's not like we can say we met while picking out apples in the produce section at the grocer or while standing in line at the post office."

Raine could see how their meeting could be a problem to explain. He didn't know if Missy had kept him secret. "Who else knows about the scam and that I'm the soldier in the photo?"

Missy knew Raine deserved a more complete explanation regarding the scam. "The only person I ever told about the scam is my best friend Dotty. I was so excited about your arrival; I told her you were here. I've kept her in the loop about you and our tours the last two days. Dotty is in her late seventies, lives alone, and doesn't have any hobbies other than me. She sort of lives vicariously through me.

169

Her greatest asset is being a sounding board for me, so I don't go off the rails. In the case with the scammer, I kinda did. She's been concerned about my safety physically and mentally ever since the scam started.

I'm glad the scam started and has now ended with finding you. I'd like us to be friends and more, but I'm fairly settled in life and your life is up in the air. I don't know how you feel about us and what you want."

Once again Missy had been rattling on just like Dotty and was afraid Raine would be confused by what she said. He had become important to her, and she didn't want to mess it up. She hoped Raine would understand her intentions.

Raine had been thinking about the same thing. He had called his dad to let him know he was spending some time in the Pacific Northwest but hadn't mentioned his involvement with Missy. She was right, how was he going to explain his new relationship to his dad and friends.

"You're right, our meeting is one for the books, but I don't care. No matter what brought us together, I'm glad it happened too. My dad and friends won't care either once they meet you. At first our friends will have a lot of questions and you're right it will be difficult to explain meeting through a scam.

We could just limit the story to the day you notified the army recruiter about a scam you uncovered about a soldier who was having his identity used. Unless you want to there's no need to elaborate about the entire scam and how long it went on. I for one am grateful to you for going to the recruiter. What do you want to say about our meeting?"

"Pop-ups come on the computer all the time and that's how I first encountered the scammer. I don't want to make something up. It would only lead to problems. I'm perfectly comfortable telling people I discovered the use of your identity by a scammer in a pop-up and felt you needed to be aware this was happening. I'm comfortable with telling people the recruiter notified you.

Everyone knows I have a soft spot for injustice of all types. I was with Dotty when I stopped in at the recruiter office and that's my story. I'm with you, I don't care how we met. I'm just glad we did."

After finishing the leftover lunch, tidying the cabin, and packing the car, Missy and Raine started the drive home. When the road straightened out Missy looked over at Raine who was very quiet. He had fallen asleep. She was so pleased he could be that comfortable and relaxed with her to sleep in the car.

The day must have been successful if he was this tired. The night he fell asleep on the couch came to mind and she began to think what it would be like to sleep beside him.

She quickly tried to put the thought out of her head. He seemed to like her, but he was at loose ends. The few days they had spent together were not enough to form a lasting relationship. She said to herself 'just enjoy his company for as long as he stays you silly girl.' Those thoughts were still in her head when she pulled into the driveway of her home.

Raine woke up when she turned off the engine. "Sorry, I wasn't much of a traveling companion sleeping like that. I guess my nodding off was from the sun and all the exercise I got today."

Missy tried to hide her thoughts and the hope he would come into the house instead of getting in his car and driving to the motel.

Raine was having similar thoughts wanting to stay with Missy, but knew it was too soon and he needed to be the gentleman Missy deserved. They hadn't said anything more to one another beyond just being friends. As much as he didn't want to, he needed to get in his car and go to the motel.

Before getting out of Missy's car he asked, "Do you want me to help you unload the car before I leave?"

Reluctantly, Missy told him, "No, there isn't that much. Come for breakfast in the morning. I have an idea for a tour that will give you an even better view of the area. We're going up to Hurricane Ridge for a hike. The trail is about five miles long and there's a view of Mt. Olympus and Vancouver Island.

This will be a new adventure for me. I've never been up there. None of my friends are into hiking. If we are on a trail it's usually atop a horse. I'll make lunch for us and put it in a backpack."

Raine was starting to feel like more than a visitor with a tour guide and wanted Missy to know it. "You're quite the tour guide and not what I expected when I rang your cowbell. Our time together is more than great tours."

Raine knew he had to leave, but leaned over and gave Missy a quick kiss before getting out of the car. Missy sat in the car for several minutes stunned, but excited by the kiss.

Chapter 24

The breakfast menu for this trip needed to be something that would stay in their tummies and keep them warm. Missy had just the right dish in mind. The cowbell rang and Raine walked in. He put his arm around Missy and kissed her saying, "Good morning sunshine. What's on the breakfast menu this morning with the woman who says she doesn't know how to cook?"

"Well, good morning to you too. That kiss just made my day and I can't cook, just make a good breakfast and bake delicious cookies."

Raine was hoping he hadn't been too forward with the kiss, which was why he decided to defuse what could be an awkward moment by teasing Missy about her cooking. "Breakfast is a good start to my day and I do like a late-night cookie snack. Maybe I can fill in the middle. I know how to cook. Nothing fancy, but I can grill a great steak."

Missy thought about that, "Sorry, I don't have a grill. You may be stuck with take-out."

Raine had a solution, "No problem, they sell them in stores, and you have a really nice covered porch that would be perfect for one."

Missy wanted to see just how committed he was about staying in Sequim and continuing their friendship, so she asked, "I guess this means you're going to start cooking. That's what you get for being a smart aleck. Maybe we can put your skills to the test tomorrow.

Today I have a full day planned for us. This morning we're going to have mega oatmeal because we'll need lots of energy. It's loaded with dried fruit, pecans and apples. I've also added some brown sugar. We need a good fortifying breakfast."

Fortification was what Raine was needing all right, but for a different reason. The tours with Missy were working out just fine and he wanted to make some plans for her. Without knowing it she had given him more than a few enjoyable days. For the first time in a long time, his future was starting to form. The last few years he avoided planning for the future. It was just too daunting. All of his adult life was in the military and retirement after leaving the service almost frightened him.

The drive to the ridge trailhead was a long and winding road. There were some great views along the way, but Raine was on the shoulder side of the car which had a view of the hillside, so Missy stopped at a few pullouts. As they stood at the railings, Raine put his arm around Missy to shield her from the cool breeze. His touch was a welcome sensation. This was starting to feel much more to Missy than the thoughts she had for the soldier in the photo.

What was she going to do if he went away, and she never saw him again? He seemed to like the Pacific Northwest, but she didn't know if he liked the area and her enough to stay.

Raine was trying to figure out his feelings for Missy, where his future was headed, and what he was going to do about it. This was the first time he had a definite option since his last day in the army. The days with Missy were different from the days he had spent with other women. Maybe it was because before he always knew he would be moving on to another assignment and didn't let himself get involved. Now he could stay if everything worked out the way he wanted.

They started the hike and talked along the way, mostly about the scenery, both avoiding their thoughts about each other from the drive up the mountain. When they reached the trail end, lunch was definitely needed. Missy had packed apples, cheese wedges, crackers, her chocolate chip cookies, and water.

Raine pulled the backpack off, and they prepared the lunch on a bench overlooking the valley below. It reminded Raine of the first walk with Missy at the spit when they sat on a bench that overlooked the farmland. Had he known he would feel this way about Missy then? He knows exactly how he feels now, and he was ready to make his plans.

The hike back to the trailhead was quiet except for Missy's explanation of tomorrow's venture. "We're going to Cape Flattery. It is the most northwestern part of the US. I made arrangements for a permit from the Makah reservation museum to park at the trailhead. This is one of my favorite places to visit. You'll love it."

Raine was thinking, 'I'm beginning to love something more than just the places we visit.' He was also thinking about what he wanted to do when they returned to town.

Part way back to town Missy stopped at another scenic viewpoint. Raine made a request, "How about I drive the rest of the way home? It's been a long trip and I'd like to give you a break."

Missy liked the idea Raine would want to drive. She was concerned he might feel strange being chauffeured around by a woman. She liked a man who was dominant, yet not possessive. Besides, she didn't want Raine to only see her as a tour guide. It was time he was able to make some decisions about their time together.

Having a woman controlling a man's life was a sure way to disaster. Not only would his ego be deflated, but he would eventually want to escape. If she wanted to know more about this man, she had to let him show who he was. She gladly handed the keys to Raine and climbed into the passenger seat.

Once they entered town, Raine chose a different route than the one to Missy's house. His stomach had started to growl from hunger, and he put his plan into motion.

"That was a nice lunch, but it's long gone now. On my trips to and from the motel, I remember seeing a Home Depot and Safeway. I'm taking charge of the rest of our day. They sell grills at Home Depot, and we can get steaks and potatoes to grill at Safeway. You wanted to see my cooking skills and I'm ready to step up."

Missy had a thought, "Raine you'll need more than cooking skills. Won't the grill need to be assembled?"

"Missy, I'm an engineer, no problem."

Raine was true to his word. In no more than twenty minutes the grill was assembled and heating up. Missy sliced some tomatoes to go with the steaks and potatoes. This was the best dinner yet for the two. It seemed like they were a normal couple living a normal life.

The strange beginning of their relationship was dissolving away for both of them. Missy was thrilled Raine was making decisions for them. She wanted him to feel like he was making plans for their time together too.

There was still one uncomfortable situation that was once again popping up. It was when the evening ended and Raine had to go back to the motel. It was getting more and more difficult for him to say goodnight. Every time he returned to the empty motel room it seemed even more lonely. Missy was having the same feelings. She would look down at Puffy and realize how empty her life felt with just a dog for company. She had been living alone for so long, life with the dog had been enough until now.

Dotty's warning about becoming too attached to Raine was prudent. She would like a life with Raine, but what did he want? It seemed as though he really liked her, and she certainly liked him.

How long would it take until either she or he would be brave enough to reveal their feelings? They had only known each other for a few days. Is that long enough for them to truly know if they want a

lasting relationship? Can two people from dissimilar backgrounds and different places in their lives come together? These questions were driving Missy crazy, but her belief in life was if it is meant to be, it will happen. She decided to stay positive.

Chapter 25

Breakfast for today was coffee and pastries to go. They needed an early start for the long drive to Cape Flattery. During the drive Missy made a few stops at some of the beaches and other points of interest that might be fun for future trips. She was hoping Raine would mention something about what he wanted to do for his future, but he didn't.

She had great difficulty figuring out what his plans were and wasn't secure enough to ask him. There was a fear she would be disappointed if the answer wasn't what she wanted. This was not the norm for her. She was usually much bolder and spoke her mind. Why was she so hesitant with Raine?

What Missy didn't know was Raine wasn't concerned about future trips to interesting places. He was thinking about the big picture for the next phase of his life and how he was going to include Missy. There were so many things he needed to do. He didn't even have a vehicle and had never bothered to plan for a house as a permanent place to live after he retired.

All his belongings, which wasn't much, were stored at his dad's house where he stayed when on leave. His life in the military was like a vagabond moving from one station to another. He hadn't put down roots anywhere. It was time to make a new life for himself and he wanted Missy to be part of it. How was he going to make this happen? Missy already had a life that seemed to be working just fine for her. Would she want to include him in her life?

All of these questions were starting to torture him and prevent his enjoyment of the ventures with Missy. Things had to change, and it was up to him to start making the life he wanted. He knew what he needed to do, and this day was going to be the beginning. All of a sudden he woke out of his doubts and a huge smile came across his face.

Missy looked over at the grin on Raine's face and asked, "Why the grin. Am I missing something?"

Raine decided to reveal some of his thoughts, "No, I'm just enjoying the drive and the time we're spending together. Just sitting here watching you and listening to your voice makes me happy. I never gave much thought to how I would respond to leaving the military. I just knew it was time.

You've given me a lot to think about. You're a bright and exciting woman and I think your enthusiasm for life is rubbing off on me. That's one of the problems with military life. There isn't much that's exciting or fun. Being with you and the fun we're having has made a profound change for me. I want you to know how much I appreciate everything we're doing together."

Hearing this was just what Missy needed to express her feelings. "Raine, I'm having just as much fun. My life is usually such a rut. Every day is the same. I take care of my animals and play with them. I visit Dotty, call some of my friends, work on my novel, and play golf. Meeting you and running around to the places I think will be of interest to you has been a welcome change."

Raine patiently listened thinking, 'maybe Missy's life isn't as complete as I thought it is.'

I want more out of life than a comfortable existence. I want adventures and fun. I was stuck like you when I felt compelled to stay with my parents and help run the hotel. It consumed most of my life and I haven't been brave enough to venture out on my own. I was even grounded to the farm when I got married.

My life has been so much fun since you rang my cowbell. Having you come into my life has changed things for me and I think for the better. Our trips together have given me hope that I can work on some new adventures."

Raine was hearing just what he was hoping, "Missy, I have a feeling life with you is going to be an adventure."

Wow, thought Missy, the phrase 'life with you is' was just what she wanted to hear. Now she was the one with a grin on her face.

That smile stayed on Missy's face all the way to the museum where she picked up the parking pass and continued on to the parking lot at the trailhead. The walk on the cedar plank trail was fun. They explored all three platforms and ate their lunch watching the waves crash on the rocks below. The views were stunning and worthy of several photos. It was a beautiful and warm early summer day, just the perfect type made for two people to grow their feelings for one another.

Once again Raine drove on the trip back to town. He was also thinking about dinner and suggested they search for some fresh seafood he could cook on their new grill.

Missy put on her thinking cap, "I think I remember a fish market on the highway going through PA. What do you have in mind?"

"Let's see if we can find the market and buy what's fresh. I want something I can cook on our grill. I'm game for anything except maybe octopus. That would gross me out and I have a feeling it's not on your list of acceptable food either."

Missy grimaced, "You're right about that. I have the makings of a salad and some frozen garlic bread to go with the fish. I like our meals at home that we make together."

Raine picked up on the word 'home' and once again he had that grin on his face. Yeah, that was what he wanted - a home with the woman he was falling in love with.

Luck was with them and the fish market was open. The freshest fish happened to be salmon, which would be great on the grill.

Dinner was perfect and enjoyable. After clearing the dishes, they sat on the porch with a glass of wine watching the sunset. As the evening cooled Raine could see Missy was getting cold, so he suggested they go inside and finish watching the sunset on the couch. Once again the evening ended with the same situation. This time Raine couldn't face going back to the motel.

He leaned over and kissed Missy, "The minute you opened your door and stood there in shock at seeing me, my life changed. I didn't have any idea why I couldn't just turn and walk away after thanking you for your tenacity in locating me with the information about the scam. There was something about the encounter that made me want to get to know you. Every time I thought it was time to say thank you and leave, I couldn't do it.

When you suggested the coffee, I thought that was reasonable. Then you invited me for dinner. By that time there was no way I would walk out the door. Now I'm falling in love with you, and I don't want to walk out that door alone again."

Missy sat in silence stunned, way more than excited that he said he was in love with her.

Raine wanted her to know, "Every day we've spent together has convinced me we can be happy and have a great life. I know our lives are completely different. You're settled here and I'm living out of a suitcase. I don't have anything to offer you except for my love. I'm not without means, I have a liberal retirement from the army and have invested well over the years. I just don't have much in the way of material things. I don't even own a car."

Missy was overjoyed to hear that Raine loved her, so she returned the kiss. "I don't care about material things. All I need is a man who loves me that I can love in return. It's a challenge for two people our age who have lived different lives, but that will keep us working together to figure it out. If life was easy, it would be boring."

Now it was Raine's turn to sit and listen. Yes, Missy had kissed him, and she professed her love. Thank God he rang her cowbell.

"Mostly we have to learn to talk to each other about our feelings and what we want out of life. From that we can build a relationship. Our friendship is different for me because I was aware of you for so long. I know this is going to sound weird, but when I was playing the game with the scammer I wrote something to him as a way to string him along. As I wrote it I thought about you, and wished I was saying this to you.

This is what I wrote: 'These are the things that are important to me. Staying close to your friends, walking on the beach holding hands, a snuggle with your best friend as a perfect end to the day, the look on your face that says you're all I will ever need and want, a spontaneous compassionate gesture, the ability to laugh at yourself, and wanting to give more than receive.' I want these things with you."

Raine kissed Missy holding her so tight she was almost out of breath.

He looked at her and said, "All those things would make me the luckiest and happiest man on the planet. I feel all of that for you and I know you feel it for me. The thought of going back to the motel tonight is killing me."

Missy was having the same feelings and said, "Then stay," as she reached to unbuckle his belt. It was a rush to see who could undress the other first and they fell into each other even though it had been ages for each of them. They were so eager to express their love for one another that it seemed natural and felt perfect.

As they laid wrapped together Missy told Raine, "When we took our first tour on the spit and sat on the bench a feeling came over me. It was an overwhelming and completely consuming feeling of happiness. It was like having a warm blanket folded around you. That was when I started falling in love with you. From that time on I was hopelessly in love."

Raine knew when love happened for him, "I think love happened for me the minute you opened the door and said - "Oh my God, you're real."

Missy laughed, "You remember that. I felt so dumb for saying it. I had no way of knowing if the information I gave the recruiter would ever reach you. Considering the circumstances of my involvement with the scammer, I guess you understood."

Rain confessed, "I thought you were really cute and funny. Now I can see there is so much more to you that I love. Every day I discover all kinds of things I love about you, and I can't wait to learn more."

Eventually exhaustion took over and they snuggled into sleep. The only one who wasn't happy was Puffy who had been relegated to her doggie bed on the floor.

Chapter 26

This time Raine was thrilled to go back to the motel. He was going to check out and stay with Missy in what would be their home. They would work together to see if life with each other would be what they wanted. While Raine was gone Missy made room for him with an empty dresser drawer and space in the closet. She wanted him to feel at home in her house.

The other thing she had to do was return all the missed calls from Dotty. What was she going to say? Dotty had been so concerned about Missy's inclusion of Raine in her life. Maybe if she met him, she would understand the attraction she had to Raine.

So much had happened so quickly since Missy opened her door that afternoon. She and Raine had only been together a few days. Was that enough time to know a person sufficiently to have him share her home? Dotty was continuously warning her about being naive and vulnerable.

Missy's thoughts went to the escapade with the scammer that turned dangerous, and he was probably on the other side of the world.

This was a real man who she was inviting into her home. Right or wrong, she was in love, wanted a life with him, and this was the choice she made. Would Dotty chastise her again or be pleased she was happy and had a man in her life?

There was only one way to find out, and she made the call, "Hi Dotty, once again I have to apologize for not getting back to you."

Dotty had her suspicions why Missy had been MIA, "You've been spending all your time with that man haven't you?"

"Guilty as charged, but wait till you meet him," admitted Missy. "You'll see why. He's wonderful and I'll come right out with it. We've fallen in love and he's moving into my house today."

Dotty only had one thing to say,

"Wait just a minute. I need to get a long drink of something very alcoholic." Several minutes later Dotty finally returned to the phone. "I knew this was going to happen. When you didn't return my many, many calls, I had my suspicions. My guess is that he has already been in your bed."

With that statement, Missy was again silent.

Dotty evidently was not finished, "This is exactly what I was afraid of. From the day you told me he showed up at your house, I knew you were in trouble. This goes back to all those times you were looking at the photo from the scammer. I knew you were too attracted to him even before he came here. What am I going to do with you? Bring this man over here today so I can make up my mind whether to commend you or lock you up."

Missy had to laugh. It was nice that Dotty was concerned for her safety, mentally and physically. She suspected there was another reason for wanting to meet Raine. Dotty liked men and would take any opportunity to engage with them. Now that Missy had fallen for this man, Dotty would definitely have to see him and judge for herself. Knowing Dotty and her preferences, Raine was probably not her first choice based on his looks. Dotty liked big husky men and Raine was slim.

Missy had to think for a minute. "I'm going to have to run this by Raine. I don't know how well he will take to being put on the spot like that. I can only imagine the third degree you will come up with for him. He needs to be prepared for the inquisition that you'll give him.

He knows you were complicit with my involvement in the scam, that I've told you he's here, and I've been giving him a tour of the peninsula. You're my best friend and I do know you have my interests at heart. I want a relationship with Raine, and I want you to be okay with it."

"Missy, I've known you for what seems like forever and if he makes you happy, then I'm happy too," conceded Dotty. "I guess if you've developed more than strong feelings for him over the few days you've spent together then there must be some redeeming qualities in him."

Dotty wasn't going to take Missy's choice lightly. She stood her ground, "I reserve the right to my opinion about him and you know I will speak my mind. I'll try to be polite and not grill him to death."

Missy knew better, "Give me a break Dotty, you will scrutinize every aspect of him. I'll give him fair warning and let him decide when he's ready to measure up for your approval. Let's meet for the talk this afternoon. Raine and I don't have any plans for today. I'll give you a call before we come over."

The greeting Raine got from Missy upon his return from the motel started great. She gave him a passionate kiss and put a welcome sign with red paper hearts on the bed. "Hi, I've made some room for your things. Let's get them put away and then we need to have a little chat."

Raine's face showed concern, "I'm confused. Ordinarily I'd be slightly unsettled at a phrase like 'we need to have a little chat', but you have a smile on your face."

Missy felt she needed to reassure Raine, "Don't worry everything is fine, we talked about this. You remember me telling you about my friend Dotty? Well, while you were checking out of the motel, I returned her many calls from the last few days. I filled her in on our activities and she wants to meet you."

Raine was starting to feel unsettled. "From what you've told me about Dotty, I have a feeling it's going to be an interrogation."

Missy knew she would soon be introducing Raine to her friends, and Dotty would be the most challenging.

"Dotty is my closest and oldest friend. You need to be aware Dotty is very good at speaking her mind and doesn't miss words. There isn't anyone sweeter than Dotty when you get to know her. She is very protective and knows more about me than anyone."

Raine was beginning to see there could be an advantage to meeting Dotty since he wanted to know more about the woman he had fallen in love with.

"When is this interrogation, um, I mean meeting with Dotty going to take place?"

"Why don't we get it out of the way this afternoon." Raine could hear some hesitation in Missy's voice.

Once again Raine was unsettled, "From the way you say that I get the feeling you aren't looking forward to this either. Can you give me a heads up? Just exactly what have you told Dotty?"

Sheepishly Missy confided, "Like I said, Dotty knows me very well. She's very good at reading between the lines of what I say or don't say."

Raine had his suspicions, "So she knows we slept together last night even though you didn't tell her we did."

Keeping the sheepish look Missy confessed, "Yeah."

Raine laughed and couldn't resist teasing Missy, "Okay then, now I guess I'll have to marry you."

Missy had to laugh too but was shocked that he would bring up marriage.

"Don't worry, Dotty doesn't own a shotgun. You'll be perfectly safe. I think we should have lunch first. You'll need sustenance to make it through an afternoon with Dotty. Visits with her are never short. Calling her a chatterbox is an understatement. Besides all of the questions she'll bombard you with, you'll be examined from the top of your head to your feet."

Raine gave that some thought. "In that case I should probably rethink my wardrobe. What type of attire would please Dotty?"

Missy gave Raine a once over and told him, "You'll look great in anything you wear. Don't worry."

Raine grinned and reassured Missy, "I'm not worried. I want to meet all your friends. Each one of them will give me more insight as to who you are and why I've fallen in love with you."

Missy told him, "We'll start with Dotty. I'd love to have all my friends meet you and I'm sure they'll think you're the perfect man for me, because I think you are. If you pass with Dotty which I'm sure you will, it will be clear sailing from then on. I want to meet all the people in your life too."

They had talked about meeting each other's friends and what they planned to say. This would be different since Dotty knew the whole story. Missy was right, meeting Dotty first was best. Sort of testing the waters.

The time had come, so Raine and Missy piled into her car and headed to Dotty's house. Raine already had a plan for the meeting. He had been trained in interrogation techniques and was sure he could match Dotty with no problem.

He announced, "I'd like to make a stop at Safeway before we get to Dotty's house. I need something to disarm her with. A nice bouquet of flowers should do the trick. What woman doesn't like to have a man give her flowers?"

Missy was slightly shocked, "You're using military tactics to win over Dotty?"

Defending his plan of action, he explained, "I'm not letting nearly forty years of training go to waste. Besides, I'm already at a disadvantage."

"What do you mean?" asked Missy.

Raine expressed what he was thinking, "You and Dotty have been best friends for years right? Don't you think she's going to be upset that you might have a new best friend - me? I want to make her feel she will always be included in our friendship."

Missy was blown away and Raine would be that considerate. "You never cease to amaze me. Are you sure you're real?"

"What can I say, my grandmother raised me right."

"Yes, indeed she did, and I owe her thanks for more than your manners," conceded Missy. "The flowers are a nice touch, but I'm sure Dotty will melt at the sight of you just like I did the day you rang my cowbell."

"You melted?"

Missy tilted her head like a shy schoolgirl, "Yeah, melted, swooned and nearly fainted."

"Wow, and I didn't even bring you flowers." Raine wanted to know, "What made you 'melt'?

"The uniform with your name on it did for me."

"I'll put it on for you anytime you want if we can have another encounter like last night again."

"Mister, I prefer you without it or anything actually," said Missy with a seductive look on her face.

With an attempt to regain composure Raine told her, "Stop it or I'm going to turn this car around. Right now, I need to be all business. I have to get my game face on."

Missy was right. Dotty took one look at Raine, and she melted, or it could have been the libation she had consumed to ready herself for the meeting. He may not be the build and type of man she prefers, but his smile did the trick. She was the perfect hostess and gushed over the flowers.

It was all Missy could do not to laugh at the performance Raine put on. He was way beyond the perfect gentleman and Dotty was eating out of his hand. Who knew she was that into men. If Dotty were younger, she would have given Missy a run for her money.

Unfortunately, either the alcohol effects ran out or Dotty came to her senses, because the inquisition started in earnest.

"I assume Missy told you about our venture with the scammer. Missy and I had that guy's number from the beginning. He couldn't pull anything over on us. We gave him a good run for his money."

Raine refrained from the smirk he wanted to display and let Dotty rattle on as Missy assured him she would.

"I'm sure you can tell by looking at me, I wasn't born yesterday. You think you can come in here with flowers and sweet talk to easily win me over? What are your intentions for my friend, young man?"

Both Raine and Missy couldn't help squashing the need to laugh and tried their best to just smile.

Raine was ready, "Dotty, I like that you come right to the point. I can tell you're a woman who knows her own mind and isn't afraid to speak it. I respect that. You and Missy have been friends for a long time and I'm grateful that you're looking out for her. Now I'll be here to help you with that task. I have a feeling keeping Missy on the straight and narrow will require both of us."

Missy was feeling slighted so she spoke up, "Wait a minute, why do you two think I need both of you looking after me?"

Dotty had the answer, "After the debacle with the scammer and your whirlwind romance with Raine, can you seriously ask that?"

Raine came to the defense of Missy and answered Dotty's question. "From the moment Missy opened her door to me, I was attracted to her. I was the one who suggested the tour guide ventures. We both enjoyed the time we spent getting to know each other. I love Missy and I intend to make sure we spend the rest of our lives together. I'll do whatever it takes to make her the happiest woman on the planet."

Dotty's mouth was wide open, and for the first time Missy could think of, there were no words coming out. Finally, she spoke, "You better make her happy buster or I'll use my cane to break both your legs." Now they were getting the true Dotty.

All three of them laughed and Raine had definitely won over Dotty. Hopefully, all the berating for Missy's misadventures would stop. The only problem was Dotty had resumed her nonstop conversation technique. They had to get her to quit talking so they could leave.

Raine invited Dotty to dinner so he would be able to put the new grill to use again. That seemed to satisfy her enough to let them head for home with a quick stop at Safeway again for steaks.

Dinner with Dotty went well. There was only polite conversation that

didn't involve any interrogation of Raine. Dotty was her sweet self and obviously quite taken by Raine who once again turned on the charm. He started teasing Dotty about being Missy's protective sister although she was easily old enough to be Missy's mother. Dotty was just as adept at teasing Raine and Missy. It was fun for Missy to sit back and enjoy the banter.

The evening was also a relief for Missy. She had worried about including Raine in her life, but he seemed to be inserting himself with ease. Missy had to continually remind herself they just met even though she had thought about him for months while looking at his photo on her phone.

Dotty very politely made her exit after dinner at an early hour for her. Her evenings usually ended at about one AM, so ten o'clock was due only to good manners.

Missy felt the need to commend Raine on his successful charm of Dotty. "Thank you for tolerating Dotty. I know she's an acquired taste and can dominate the conversation. She tends to rattle on repeating things."

"Missy, she's a sweet lady and I find her stories funny and interesting.

She's led an amazing life sailing around the world for ten years. If her husband could put up with her on a sixty-foot sailboat for that amount of time, we can surely spend an evening with her.

There's no doubt she's crazy about you. I have to thank her for supporting you during the scam episode. I'm also glad you had her to confide about me. You're a very smart independent woman, but everyone needs someone's shoulder to lean on. Now she'll have to share her shoulder, because mine is yours." To lighten what he was saying, he added, "Besides, she loves animals so she can't be all that bad."

Chapter 27

With the two major events, Raine's move into Missy's house and his meeting with Dotty over, it was time to relax with a glass of wine. The hour was late, but that didn't matter. They both needed some quiet time.

Raine decided to continue teasing Missy, "Do I need to put on my uniform to get your full attention tonight?"

"Why bother, I'd just have to take it off."

Raine grinned, "I like the way you think. Race you to the bedroom." Intimacy was natural and easy for them. The most enjoyable part for both was snuggling together after. Last night they fell asleep quickly, but tonight they were still wound up after the meeting with Dotty and lay awake.

Missy rolled over against Raine as he lay on his back. She ran her hand over his stomach to his side and felt the scar on his waist. There was a question she wanted to ask, "When we were at the lake, I couldn't help noticing all the scars on your back and side. I didn't say anything. I was afraid it would bring up some bad memories of something that happened in the war. I wanted you to have a fun day, so I kept it to myself."

Raine knew he would eventually need to explain the scars, "Oddly enough I don't have any bad memories of the scars. I don't have any memory at all. It was early in the 1990's when I was in Kuwait. We were in a jeep transport just outside a village. I was sitting on the tailgate watching our six. We hit an IED, and I was blown off the back.

About a week later I woke up lying on my side in a hospital in Germany. I had shrapnel cuts in my back and a hole through my side. I must have had my helmet unbuckled because I was hit in the back of my head and had a gash in my scalp."

Missy suppressed a gasp but couldn't help feeling for Raine as there was a pained expression on his face.

"I was so dizzy and incoherent; it was about a month before I could function properly. It took a lot of physical and mental therapy to get my head and body straightened out. I was lucky because most TBI's, traumatic brain injuries, are career ending. I guess the army thought my engineering skills were valuable because they promoted me to lieutenant and gave me supervisory appointments in areas without active combat.

My jobs were to design and oversee the construction of bridges and reconstruction of blown out buildings, mostly hospitals and schools. Either we or the enemy, whoever it happened to be at the time, blew them up and we rebuilt them. I spent over twenty years in war zones as a soldier and never fired my gun at the enemy.

I'm glad I didn't have to kill anyone, but I saw a lot of people on both sides get killed. I don't really have PTSD like a lot of guys. I get some flashbacks, but that's all. I'm proud of my service and glad I did it. That life is behind me now and I want to start a new chapter. A new chapter with you and the life we build together. Speaking of together," with that Raine pulled Missy against him and stopped talking.

Morning came with a heavy fog bank covering the valley below the house. The summer fog banks that roll in from the ocean quite often crept into the valley. After breakfast Raine and Missy sat on the couch watching the fog roll through and waiting for the sun to warm their day. Sitting with Raine like this was something Missy wanted to last forever. He mentioned a new chapter for his life with her they would build together.

She had to know if this could be her life, so she asked a huge question. "Raine, have you decided what you want to do for the rest of your life? You mentioned not wanting a full-time career. What other interests do you have?"

It took Raine a minute to answer. Not because he had to think what to say, but because he wanted to say so much. Before meeting Missy, he hadn't given his future much thought. The Army had been his whole life and leaving it was daunting. He was now interested in exploring a life of leisure to see how that felt.

In the last few days, he decided on the one thing he wanted for the future. "I don't care what I do with the rest of my life as long as I do it with you. No matter where or how I spend my life doesn't matter. The future just has to have you in it.

My life hasn't been perfect. We've talked some about our childhoods and other parts of our lives, but there's more. There are some holes in my life I've filled in, but there are a few left to deal with. I want you to know who and why I'm the man sitting here. I don't want any questions between us. We need to be completely honest with each other."

What Raine was saying concerned Missy, but she waited to hear him tell her more. This seemed to be something essential to Raine.

"We need to go to Connecticut so you can meet my dad. It's important for him to know I've found someone to love. I need to tell you why.

There's something I want to tell you about me. It's been on my mind lately knowing how much I've come to love you. I love my dad, but there's been a strain in our relationship. He blames himself for my staying in the service and living alone without a woman to love. It's not his fault. I just never remained stationed in one place long enough to build a relationship with a woman. Frankly, I wasn't good at relationships."

This last statement puzzled Missy. She thought their relationship formed easily. Why didn't Raine think he wasn't good at relationships? Would that be a sign theirs was doomed?

"Raine, do you have any doubts about our relationship? I know we've only been together a short time, but I feel we have a strong connection."

For a moment Raine saw his confession was causing Missy to worry.

"My future with you is solid. There's just a few things I need to put to rest. I want to be the man you deserve. What I need to clear up is with my dad and the relationship we have.

When we got to Connecticut and I started high school, I began having feelings for a girl I was dating. My dad sat me down for what I thought was a birds and the bees talk. What he told me changed my life and has stayed with me until now that I met you.

Remember when we were sitting on the bench at the spit, and you asked me about my childhood? I told you I liked to think my mother's death was an accident. That's what I like to think, but I'll never know for sure. There was more to it."

Once again Missy was eager to learn more about the man she had fallen into love with, so she sat quietly and let him continue.

"This is what my dad told me that day. What my grandmother said about my mother was right and more. She liked to party and have sex with lots of boys including my dad. Her parents kicked her out when she got pregnant. My dad was the one who stood up to his responsibility and married her to give the baby a name. He loved her even with her wild ways. He said she was sweet, beautiful, and full of life.

When the baby came, me, she was the perfect mother at first. She would sit for hours and rock and sing to me. But that didn't last. When I was only a few months old, my grandmother had to start taking care of me. My mom started going out at night and wouldn't come home until early morning. I don't know how my dad was able to stay with her knowing what she was probably doing. I think it was only because of me. He wanted me to have a normal life with a mother and father. Maybe he hoped she would stop someday. She did, but not in the way he expected. She finally ended up in the ravine.

What my dad told me next is what changed everything between us. The medical examiner found she was pregnant. It wasn't my dad's because she made him have a vasectomy after I was born. She didn't want any more children. I don't think she ever wanted me.

But that wasn't the worst thing he told me. My grandmother thought he wasn't my father because he and my mother had brown eyes and mine are blue. That doesn't always hold true, but she believed it. He wanted me to know he might not be my biological father and I might not know for sure.

He'd never talked about my mother before. All I knew was my grandmother saying she was a party girl and died when her car went into the ravine. As far as I'm concerned he's my dad and always will be, but I didn't know who I was considering the type of woman my mother was. Also, what if he wasn't my real father, who was? I was a confused mess trying to deal with that question.

That was when I decided to enlist in the Army; I needed an identity. That's probably why I was so concerned about the scam. My identity was so much of a question, I didn't want someone soiling it. I felt violated even more about the scam, than I did with what my dad told me."

'So, it wasn't just a thank you that brought Raine to my doorstep. The scam was personal to him as well', thought Missy.

"When DNA became available I had to know who I was or wasn't. He's not my dad, but I love him, and I'll never tell him what I know. I want you to know this because in the past it held me back in relationships.

For so many years I didn't know who I was and had so many conflicted feelings about my parents. I was afraid I couldn't accept someone else if I couldn't accept myself. It's taken me a long time, but I've come to terms with my paternity and accept who I am.

You'll likely pick up on the strain with my dad when you meet him, and I want you to know why. I've never told anyone this, but I love you so much I feel you need to know why you're the first woman I want to live with forever. My story isn't like a Hallmark movie, but I'm hoping the ending will be."

Missy sat quiet and let Raine continue to talk. She wanted to know as much about him as he would tell her. He said this was the first time he told anyone about his self-esteem. She was amazed he would be that open and honest. What he said made sense and also made her determined he would feel the love she had for him.

Raine didn't want Missy to think his entire life was a mess, so he told her about his dad and grandparents growing up.

"My grandfather and dad worked as carpenters and handymen. Gramps was what you would call a jack-of-all-trades. He could fix anything. We didn't have much in the way of material things and times were tough. There was always good food on the table from Gram's garden, but not much else.

My grandmother never said we were poor; she was just good at being thrifty. The only time I got new clothes was when I grew out of the patched up old ones. When I think back, my grandmother was a saint. She worked herself to the bone feeding, cleaning and caring for two men and a boy she felt wasn't her son's child.

I didn't give much thought to how they felt when my dad and I left to move to Connecticut. I just thought it would be easier for them to have two less mouths to feed.

Through the years I got plenty of letters from my grandmother and I called when I could. I never saw them again after the day we drove away. I was overseas when I got word they passed and learned how it happened.

It was something from a love story. My grandparents had a love that lasted their entire lives. They were in their nineties when my grandmother developed a brain tumor that was terminal. My grandfather and grandmother wrote a letter to my dad, laid down in bed and took lethal doses of her medication. He was healthy but couldn't live without her."

Missy choked up hearing the sad but sweet story and saw a single tear on Raine's cheek.

Raine regained his composure and continued, "The army gives you bereavement leave and pay to return home. I got a flight for my dad and me to Texas so we could close their estate. My grandmother's thrifty life left a sizable bank account.

The town had grown around their home making the lot worth enough for my dad to pay off his mortgage and retire. He and I invested the balance and he's been financially stable for the first time in his life."

As Raine talked about his grandparents, Missy could see a loving look on his face. His story of growing up without a mother was sad, but when he talked about his grandparents it seemed he was loved.

Missy assured him, "Your grandparents sound like wonderful people." She hoped he had a happy childhood like she did and wanted to ask, "Was growing up with your dad and grandparents a happy childhood?"

Raine reminisced from when he was a boy, "Yeah, I had some buddies from school to play and hang out with. When I was old enough, I worked on weekends and summers with my dad and Gramps. I learned a lot from them besides the carpentry. They gave me an allowance for my work when I was about ten and told me I could spend it or save it for something special. I saved my money for two years.

That was about the time I wanted a bike really bad, so I bought a new red Schwinn bike. I was so proud of that bike and rode it everywhere. Saving my allowance was hard to do, I remember how much I wanted to ask girls for a date but didn't have any extra money."

Missy was still curious about Raine's childhood and asked, "I bet you had a lot of girlfriends in school anyway. A nice-looking guy like you."

Raine had to admit, "No, I was too shy, and I never had a car to use for dates. It's not easy to ask a girl out for a date when you would have to pick her up in Gramp's panel truck that smelled like cigarettes and beer. Funny the things you remember. That's what I want to do next."

Missy was confused, "Buy a bike?"

Now Raine seemed very excited, "No, I want a big boy toy! I'm going to buy a truck. Maybe a shiny silver one with four-wheel drive. Can you believe I've never owned a vehicle? I've always rented one or drove my dad's when home on leave."

Not wanting Raine to get sticker shock Missy told him, "You do realize a new truck like you want costs between sixty and eighty thousand dollars. Even used they are at least fifty thousand. That's why I've held on to my truck. Tuffy's not fancy, more utilitarian, but he does the job.

If you want to buy a new truck, then that's exactly what you should do. I love truck shopping. Can I go with you?"

"Of course, and I need to turn in the rental car. It's an Enterprise car and they said I can turn it in at any dealer." Raine looked them up on his phone and saw there was one in Port Angeles. "Let's go to PA, turn in the rental car, and I saw several car dealerships when we drove through town the other day."

Raine jumped up. "Come on, we're going truck shopping."

Missy had to laugh. Raine was like the little boy getting his first bike.

"Well, you won't have to worry about dating now. You can pick me up for a date in the shiny new truck you want to buy."

At the third dealership Raine saw the truck of his dreams. It was a Chevy Silverado 2500 crew cab, four-wheel drive in the exact shiny silver color he wanted. Better yet it was used with low mileage and at a reasonable price. It took over an hour of negotiating, but Raine was finally handed the keys. After they dropped off the rental car, he drove Missy home in his shiny very first vehicle.

Chapter 28

T he first thing Raine did when they got home was leave and go to the auto parts store to equip his new toy with all the accessories he wanted to make it perfect. He returned with a bouquet of flowers for Missy.

Beaming Missy wondered, "Thank you for the flowers, but I'm not sure what the occasion is."

"This is a feeble attempt to thank you for listening to me as I spilled my guts out regarding my life. You got me thinking about a plan for the future and that led me to my truck. I really love that truck and I really love you."

Hoping he would say yes, Missy asked, "Does that mean you might let me drive your shiny new truck?"

"My truck, your truck, it's all the same to me. We're going to share everything," promised Raine. "Which brings me to something I want. It's time you spilled your guts about your childhood. I want to know who and why you're this woman."

Missy had to agree, "You're right, it's only fair. Unlike your dad, my parents were older. My mom was thirty-six when I was born and my dad four years older. As I told you before, we lived in our hotel. There were three other couples in the hotel's apartments. I never knew my grandparents. They passed when I was a baby. The occupants of one apartment were elderly and like my grandparents.

Much to my dismay, my mom insisted I was her little princess. She had me dressed in ruffles and bows until I started high school, and I insisted on being dressed like the other girls. I wasn't even allowed to wear pants until I begged them for riding lessons.

Mom took me shopping and bought me red jeans. Blue jeans were for boys, not proper girls. I guess you would have to say she was old fashioned."

Since Missy had asked him about girlfriends, Raine wanted to know about her boyfriends.

"What about boyfriends, I bet you had a lot. You had to have been very pretty even in ruffles and bows."

Admitting her shortcomings, Missy answered, "The ruffles and bows weren't much of an attraction. After I was finally dressed like the other girls there were a few, but I was too prissy for any of them to stay for long. My parents were very strict and had lots of rules. One meeting with my dad and the boy headed for the hills."

Raine was beginning to see how different their lives had been, "That must have been an education in itself growing up in a hotel with guests coming and going."

Thinking back to her childhood, Missy admitted, "It was great. The hotel was like a palace, with a stunning Victorian elegance. The lobby was magnificent. My mom was the queen of decor. Especially at Christmas. People would come just to see the elaborate decorations. There were quite a few people who stayed regularly for business or just a getaway.

The hotel was like a little city in itself. It was my whole world and I never wanted to venture away. The tenants of the apartments were an extended family. Most of them stayed with the hotel all through my childhood. I even lived at home while I went to college. My parents needed help with the hotel by then and my accounting degree came in handy.

I eventually left the hotel to explore the world outside my little circle. It took me a while, but I eventually found a guy to stick around and marry me. He was a nice man and was very good to me. The first few years were great, and I was quite happy. We worked together well, and I thought our marriage would last, but he became a closet alcoholic. There was no way to tell when he would be drunk, he hid it so well.

Our farm produced enough income for us to get by, but I think he had bigger expectations and felt he was failing. I tried to talk to him about it, but he turned into a recluse and wouldn't discuss anything. I was afraid he would end up killing someone while driving drunk, which he did too often, so I divorced him. I also feared his main interest in me was when I would inherit the hotel.

After the divorce I went back to help with the hotel. When my parents passed, living there wasn't the same without them. That's when I sold it."

Raine asked, "Is it still there?"

The sad expression on Missy's face was followed by the explanation, "No, the corporation that purchased the hotel tore it down. Like your grandparent's home the land was valuable. They did save some of the historic pieces and donated them to a museum. That's the story of my life. Pretty simple really and small compared to yours. Now I'm ready for our life and how we want to make it."

While at the auto parts store something occurred to Raine. "There is

something we need to add to our relationship. So far everything we've done has been centered on just the two of us. I have lots of friends and I'm sure you do, besides Dotty.

I've been returning calls left on my phone early in the mornings at the motel before coming to your house. My talks with friends have mostly been about my travels here without much mention about you. That has to change. I want everyone to know you. The only friend of yours I've met is Dotty and that needs to change too. What do you think?"

Missy agreed, "You're absolutely right. I've been doing the same thing. I haven't seriously talked with anyone about you because we just decided how to explain our meeting. Since most of my friends text me, it's been easy to answer with a simple text message saying, 'I've been working on my novel, need to take care of my animals, and will talk later.' It will be easier for you to meet my friends since they mostly live here and I can't wait for them to meet you. Most of my friends are paranoid about the virus and don't want to get together. My golf buddies are the only ones I regularly see in person besides Dotty."

Raine had an idea, "Okay, let's start with golf. I used to play with my dad and some of my military buddies. What about your horse friends? Dotty mentioned the horse was in a stable. Do you have friends there too?"

"I do have a horse, but I don't ride him often. I let the kids play with him. They take him on trail rides, braid his mane and tail, and spend a lot more time with him than I would. I used to keep him at home, but he's a lot happier with the other horses and kids.

Since I don't go to the stable often, I haven't made many friends there. The only ladies there are the moms of the kids and I don't have much in common with them.

I'm going to text my golf friends and set up a game. We usually play at the course just down the road. It's a flat course with wide fairways. We take our pull carts and walk. That way I can take Puffy too. I think they have loaner clubs you can use at the course. Are you ready for a game of golf?"

Playing golf seemed like an easy introduction and Raine was pleased, "I think it's a good start and will be a lot of fun. My friends live all over the world, so meeting them will be difficult. I'm going to tell them about you the next time we speak. They'll be surprised, but happy for me. We should also check on flights to Connecticut so you can meet my dad. He's been the most important person in my life and I can't wait for him to get to know you."

Chapter 29

————————————

With their resolution to open up their relationship, Raine made a flight reservation to Connecticut for the next week. Missy texted Sally and Brad with a tee time to play at their favorite course. After breakfast, the sun came out from the morning fog bank, and warmed the day for their round of golf.

The introduction of Raine to Sally and Brad was quite a surprise for them. Brad gave Raine a skeptical look and Sally was grinning side to side. As Brad and Raine led the way to the first tee, Sally whispered, "Where have you been hiding this hunk? I want the complete story as soon as we get a chance. I've been wondering why you haven't been around. Now I can see why. Is this a permanent thing?"

"I certainly hope so, he's living at my house."

Sally excitedly said, "No way, good for you girl!"

Up ahead Brad was doing his due diligence and asked, "How long have you known Missy?"

Raine could see where this was coming from and decided not to give direct answers. He didn't want to explain the way they met, "For quite sometime in a way. We've been exploring the Pacific Northwest together lately."

Brad wasn't giving up, "What type of business are you in or where do you work?"

Raine kept his answer simple, "I'm retired military, Army."

That shut Brad down for the moment and the gals caught up, so the questioning stopped. Raine was sure Brad would have more questions which was okay, and figured Brad was only looking out for Missy.

Missy and Sally teed off with their usual drives that went an average distance and were fairly close to the middle of the fairway. Brad insisted Raine tee off next. His shot went a good distance, but was just off the right side near the trees. Brad needed to outdo that shot and blasted one down the middle. Raine congratulated him and they were off. It took a couple extra shots for the gals to get to the first green. Raine's next shot landed in a sand trap and Brad's shot hit the green.

Missy walked over to Raine, "That's a huge green. Even with loaner clubs, I have a feeling you missed the green on purpose."

Raine justified his shot, "I could tell right away Brad was going to have a bit of trouble liking me. He was in that overprotective mode like a big brother. Don't worry, I'll win him over."

Missy didn't have any doubts and let him know, "Sally on the other hand is already a goner. I don't want this to go to your head, but she wanted to know where I found such a hunk."

"Really, no wonder Brad is having trouble liking me." Raine let Missy in on his plan. "I'll just keep playing my conservative game. When it's just you and me all bets are off. Even if I give you a handicap, I'll wipe your butt."

Missy liked that Raine wasn't going to be a pushover. He had an ego and needed to keep it, but she also liked his soft side. To challenge him she added, "Game on buster."

The rest of the game went well and ended with Brad and Raine becoming buddies. There were a lot of laughs, a few four-letter words, and a couple golf balls sacrificed to the water gods in the ponds near the greens. A round of beers finalized the day and a new friendship was formed. The rest of Missy's friends would learn about Raine during phone calls and emails. One by one Missy's neighbors would meet Raine in conversations over the fence. That was how most everyone chatted these days.

For Missy, meeting Raine's friends would take some time as they were scattered all over the world. The most important person for Missy to meet was Raine's father. They will be on a plane to Connecticut next week. Flying in a plane during a pandemic was not high on the list of priorities, but Raine was anxious to see his father and for the meeting with Missy.

It had been a long time since Missy had been away from home and some arrangements had to be made for the care of her animals. She was excited for another adventure and eager to meet the man from Raine's story of his childhood.

Chapter 30

Lyle Stoddard met Raine and Missy in baggage claim. Missy took one look at Lyle and knew Raine was right. This man had no resemblance to Raine whatsoever. He also looked far older than the seventy-two years he should be. He had the look of a man who led a tough life. Regardless of his appearance, Lyle was very gracious, cheerful and thrilled to see his son. Raine made the introductions and they walked to a very nice truck similar to the one Raine bought. They at least had similar tastes in vehicles.

Lyle's home was modest, but in a very nice neighborhood and well maintained. He turned out to be a very good host and made Missy feel quite comfortable. The conversation between Raine and his father was short and more like two friends talking. Raine was correct about there being a distance between him and his father. This was going to be a necessary visit for more than introducing Missy.

Dinner was steaks cooked on a grill. It was clear where Raine learned about grilling steaks. The dinner was perfect, and the evening was nice, but not like the congenial atmosphere Missy's family had.

The night at Lyle's house was a bit confusing. Lyle suspected Raine and Missy slept together, but it still seemed strange to him having Raine and Missy sleeping together in his bedroom. Missy suspected it could have been from what Raine had told her about his mother.

There were a few awkward moments, but since the house only had two bedrooms, Lyle quietly went to his room without saying anything. Raine showed Missy to what had been his bedroom since they moved to Connecticut. It was full of sports posters, trophies and everything masculine the average teenage boy would want.

Missy had to laugh realizing they were going to sleep in a double bed under a superhero bedspread. Raine made no apologies. He was just happy his father didn't object to them sleeping together.

First thing after breakfast Missy had an idea. "Raine, I'm going to the store to get the ingredients I need to prove to your dad I can make the best chocolate chip cookies he's ever tasted. Besides, I think the two of you need some time alone to talk. I can feel that strain you told me about between you and your dad."

Raine had felt the same recurring tense atmosphere that was always present when he came home on leave. "I'm sorry, and thanks for understanding. Will you be okay driving to the store and not getting lost?"

"Yeah, if I get lost I know a guy to call who can rescue me."

As soon as Missy drove away, Lyle sat down at the kitchen table where Raine was reading the paper.

"Son, I've been waiting for you to come home with a lovely woman for countless years. It took you long enough and I hope you've found what I've always wanted for you. Missy seems like a wonderful lady, and I can see how much you care for her. If she's the one, don't let her get away. My greatest hope for you is to not end up a lonely old man like me. Can you promise me that will never happen?"

Raine knew this was the time for the talk he and his dad needed, "Dad, I love Missy. She's everything I've ever wanted in a woman to spend the rest of my life with. You're right, it took me a long time to find someone. My military career always seemed to get in the way.

No, that's just the excuse I use. The truth is I had trouble finding myself and knowing who I am. It took me a long time to come to grips with the man I would be without the army. When I decided to retire there was a lot of soul searching and I learned to accept myself. I didn't know what I wanted after retiring from the army until I met Missy. Then it didn't matter what I did as long as I had her with me.

We've talked about living our lives together. That's why I brought her here so you could meet. She loves me just as much as I love her. I won't be alone Dad, but I wonder about you? Why didn't you ever marry after my mother died?"

Lyle needed to decide how to tell Raine about those years, so he didn't feel responsible. How he lived his life back then was his choice and it didn't have any reflection of Raine.

"I was eighteen with a baby and everyone in town knew about your mother and what happened to her. It was a sign hanging around my neck. I had no idea if I was your father, but you were a part of her, and I loved her despite her faults. I was determined to keep you and give you all the love I possibly could.

There was no way any woman would want to be saddled with a man who had a child, no more than a high school education, and worked for minimum wage. Especially in that town. I was lucky your grandparents took us in and helped raise you. It was all I could do to keep food on the table and give you the life I wanted you to have."

Guilt was coming over Raine as he listened to the sacrifice his dad made and how ungrateful he was to have left after high school.

Lyle explained, "Even after we moved here, I still felt tainted by the past. How could I explain what happened to your mother to another woman? I've never felt worthy after what your mother did. I've always blamed myself. There should have been something I could have done to help her.

You're the most wonderful thing to ever happen to my life. I've always wanted the best for you and I'm proud of the man you've become. My life is what I've chosen and I'm content with it. I have my home, my friends, and a good life that makes me happy."

Raine wanted to cry knowing what his father had silently dealt with all his life. It didn't matter how he was conceived or what his mother was like. Regardless of DNA this man was his father and he loved him.

He did have an identity after all. He was his father's son no matter what. All those years of feeling a loss of identity were wasted and it was time they disappeared.

This man raised him, loved him, and that was all that was important. It was time to forget the past and move forward. The past wasn't going to define him as it had his father. He was a man in love looking forward to a great life with a wonderful woman.

"Dad, I'm sorry you felt like you're not worthy of being loved. I love you, always have, and always will. Now you have Missy to love you too. You gave me the best life you could and I'm forever grateful."

Raine heard Lyle's truck return. He felt enough had been said and something positive was needed.

"Missy's back. Get your taste buds ready. Missy's claim to fame is her cookies."

The rest of the day went perfectly with lots of chocolate chip cookies to eat. Lyle did his best to embarrass Raine with stories of his childhood. There was lots of laughter and most of the emotions of the morning disappeared for Raine and Lyle. Everyone was getting a sugar high from the cookies. Lyle decided he needed a workout with the exercise equipment in his garage.

Raine drove Missy around town and showed her his high school and some of the places he used to hang out. He tried to locate some of his friends from school, but most seemed to have moved away and he lost track of them. Later the trio went to the local driving range for a challenge match between Raine and his dad. The visit was starting to be what a family should look like.

On the second night they were getting used to the double bed in Raine's bedroom and snuggled in for the night. As Raine tightly wrapped his arms around Missy, there was something different about how he held her.

"Raine what's wrong? Is it the talk you had with your dad?"

"When I enlisted, I was only thinking about myself. I wanted to change my life. To become someone else. I didn't want to be the boy with a disgraced mother and an unknown father. I didn't give a single thought about my dad. Why didn't I consider what his life had been like and would be if I enlisted and left him alone?

He must have had dreams of a future that never happened. What had his life been like? How had he dealt with a dead wife and a baby at eighteen? What effect did all this have on him? What was his life like working every job he could get at minimum wage and raising me?

'No wonder Raine is troubled,' thought Missy. That's a burden too heavy to carry.

"All these questions have been running through my head all day. I think I gave a great injustice to my dad by leaving him alone when I enlisted. When we talked today he told me he felt unworthy of being with another woman after what happened to my mother. I suspect he thinks she killed herself and he's responsible for her death.

He's been alone all these years and I never thought about how my career left him out. He gave up his future for me. A child that could have been conceived by any number of guys. He loved and raised me anyway. I've come to accept who I am and how I was raised, but now it's time I start thinking about him."

Missy was right about this visit being more than her getting to meet Raine's dad. "You were eighteen. Teenagers only think about themselves. There world is so wrapped up in what they want, it's no wonder you didn't think about your dad. You had a lot to deal with for a boy. Don't beat yourself up.

Lyle seems to have made a good life for himself. He has hobbies and buddies to play golf with. He seems content with his life. I think he's an honorable man who made the best choices he could at the time. It may not be what he originally envisioned as a boy, but I think raising you and the man you've become has made his life complete.

It may have been a rough road, but it could be that everything has turned out okay. I don't want you to think I'm making light of you and your dad's relationship. You can talk to me about your feelings toward your dad anytime. Nothing would make me happier than for you to have the type of connection you want with your dad."

Missy reflected back to her childhood for a moment and how fortunate she had been.

"It's hard for me to understand exactly how you feel. I know it's not the same as fathers and their daughters and how I was raised. Our childhoods were completely different. Hopefully, learning how your dad accepted his life will ease your mind. I want the best for both of you. For now, I think it would be good for you to sleep on it. It's been a big day."

The next morning Raine and Missy prepared for their return to Washington. Missy was thrilled to see the end of tension between Raine and his dad. The normal type of father-son rapport was very apparent. Raine seemed to have accepted the life his father led, and any apprehension was gone.

Lyle demanded Missy write out a complete recipe for the chocolate chip cookies. He was aware they could very likely add to his waistline but was willing to take the risk. He also wanted a rematch of the golf drive challenge Raine won. Plans were made for him to visit when Raine and Missy were finally settled.

The flight home was a long one. Fortunately, they got a nonstop and didn't have to hang around in an airport with hundreds of people wearing masks. Raine must have been more stressed than he let on. It wasn't too long before he was asleep in his seat. Missy looked over at him thinking the release of the strained relationship made

Missy took advantage to work on her novel that she had been neglecting ever since Raine appeared at her door. He had read the one she completed on the flight east but hadn't gotten a chance to read any of this second one. Without the use of her computer, she was writing on her tablet with a pencil. She preferred this method, but her fingers were getting tired. Soon she joined Raine for a nap.

Chapter 31

———————————

Life was working out great upon their return to Sequim. There were a few things that needed to change. One was buying a king size bed to replace the queen Missy had been holding onto for about eight years. Other than the meet and greet with the neighbors and a long visit with Dotty, small plans were beginning to form.

Both Missy and Raine were excited about their new life together. They continued visiting interesting areas on the peninsula, visiting with Chet and Carol at their lake cabin, and playing golf with Brad and Sally.

On one of the beautiful summer mornings, Missy checked her phone to see if there was a text message for a tee time. There were several text messages on the phone besides the one from Brad and Sally wanting to play golf. One text message was from an unusual number. Missy opened it and screamed, "Oh my God, no".

Raine was immediately startled, "What's wrong?"

"This is a message from the guy who was trying to scam me. I haven't had one for several months. I thought he had finally gone away."

Raine had to ask, "How do you know it's him? What did he say?"

"Because he would be the only person who would call me Julie, the name I used when I communicated with him. It just says, 'Hi Julie.' That's what he always started each text message or email with."

Raine was going to take care of the scammer once and for all, "Ignore it, and you are going to get rid of that phone number right now. Do you still have the email address?"

"I canceled the email right after I thought he went away. This really creeps me out. Why do you think he would come back after all this time?"

"Missy, do you have a record of the text messages and emails he sent you?"

Hesitating, Missy told him, "Yes, I do. I haven't told you that because I thought they would upset you. Dotty thought I should put them in one of my novels someday, so I kept a record."

Raine felt he was ready for what the scammer had done. "I appreciate you not wanting me to read them, but at this point I think I should. I might gain something from them that you missed. Maybe I can figure out why he's back. I'd like to think I can handle whatever he says."

Missy felt a bit embarrassed, "The record also includes what I said to him. Please remember it was a game and not what I really thought or felt. I wrote those things to keep the scam going and so I could trap or find him. Some of the stuff I sent was really stupid and silly."

Raine kissed Missy and said, "I don't care what you wrote. If you hadn't strung him along, we may never have met and that's the only thing important to me."

Missy pulled the folder out of her files and handed it to Raine. The look on his face told her what a mistake playing with the scammer had been. The file was over a quarter inch thick. Raine sat down and started to read. Missy worried; would he be surprised, amazed, mad, and admonish her as Dotty had done?

Halfway through reading he started to laugh just as Missy and Dotty did reading the crazy messages.

"This guy is a complete idiot. It doesn't matter that he has no clue about the military, the first problem is the fact he can't spell, and the punctuation is terrible. How could he think some woman would fall for this crap?"

Missy was relieved Raine didn't seem to be bothered by the messages the scammer sent; and didn't have anything to say about what she sent to the scammer.

"I don't know how anyone could be fooled by the stuff he wrote," admitted Missy. "Evidently some do, because he kept going and continually added more incentive. It was when he got to the point of wanting to know where I lived that I had to end it. That did scare me and now I'm scared again."

Raine's expression changed to serious when he got to the end and realized the danger this guy possessed. This was not your normal scammer who preys on lonely women. Most would move on long before this guy did when they didn't get whatever they were asking for.

Unfortunately, he couldn't determine from the messages where this guy was located other than the information Missy had uncovered.

Raine didn't know what to think about the impromptu text message that just came from the scammer. "Hopefully, shutting down the phone number will put this guy off. He's probably just playing with you. You've been adamant about never giving him anything, so there's nothing for him to gain.

From the bizarre type and length of the scam, this guy may be unstable and unpredictable. It wasn't that hard for me to find you. Granted, I had the use of military assistance, but the way technology can be used these days... We're going to be careful for a while."

Seeing the scared look on her face, Raine tried to assure Missy, "I don't think he would ever come here, and could be in some third world country."

Missy couldn't help feeling guilty. Life was turning out so great and now this problem had raised its ugly head.

"I'm so sorry this has come up. I was really stupid to get that involved with the scam and now it's come back to haunt us. I'll send messages to everyone who has my phone number and give them the new one. I don't ever want to get another message from him again. Let's not tell Dotty about this. She would be just as terrified as I am."

Even though he had his reservations Raine told her, "We'll be okay, don't worry. I'll never let anyone harm you."

Chapter 32

During the next few weeks their relationship grew even stronger. They played golf, hiked, and visited with friends who were willing to socialize. Every time a text message came on Missy's new phone number, she couldn't help hesitate. Finally, the fear left and they started making plans for a new house that would fit both their needs.

Missy's house was nice, but they needed more space to include the extra things Raine would need. Missy also felt it would be important for Raine to feel their home belonged to both of them and not just Missy. He had always lived in his family home or military homes, and it was time he had one of his own.

Raine wanted a project and that one suited him perfectly. They both had ideas for a new home, and he wanted to get them down on paper. He headed for the office supply store in town to get some graph paper. He wanted to be able to lay out a basic design for their new home.

Once again he had that excited expression of a little boy with a new toy. This was the perfect task for an engineer, and he was eager to put his knowledge to work. It must have been infectious, because Puffy jumped up wanting to go for a ride with him in the new truck.

While he was gone Missy busied herself deadheading the plants in the backyard. She heard the sound of a vehicle and looked up wondering why Raine had returned so soon. A delivery van pulled into the driveway. It wasn't the usual FedEx or UPS but did say something delivery on the side.

The fellow got out of the van, opened a side door, and stood there holding a box. The UPS man usually put packages on the front porch and drove away. She wondered why he didn't put the box down or approach her like the usual delivery men did. Did he need a signature?

This seemed odd; because of the virus, most delivery people wore masks or no longer required signatures. All the other delivery drivers kept their distance as suggested by virus precautions. The man had on a baseball cap pulled low and a scowl on his face.

Missy couldn't remember ordering anything but thought maybe Raine had. Even though she was hesitant, Missy walked up to the man who didn't smile or say anything. He just held out the box. When she took the box, her attention was taken by checking it for anything that told her where it was from.

Missy took the box and turned to walk back to the house. Before she could even think, the man grabbed her with one hand over her mouth and the other around her neck choking her. He started to drag her back to the open door on the van.

The one thought that entered Missy's head was - 'never let them take you to another location.' She had seen TV shows where a woman was abducted and raped. The message the commentator gave was - get free by any method possible. Missy was determined to not let him put her in the van.

The thing about being a woman who has outside animals is the need for a pocketknife. Missy reached around her back, grabbed the knife, and was able to open it. She had some difficulty since the knife was between her back and the front of the man. She almost had to laugh as she thought of the most likely place to stab him. A puncture in the groin did the trick. He yelled a profanity and lost his grip on her.

Missy's first thought was to run in the house, but it occurred to her he could easily break in and get her. She needed to run for help. Her most likely neighbor was Phil. He was a volunteer sheriff deputy and would have the skill to help and have a gun.

Her feet barely hit the ground as she ran, but it seemed like she was moving in slow motion. Finally, she reached Phil's door. She pounded wildly on his door, and when he opened it she almost knocked him over running inside.

She ran to his window to look up at her house and check on the delivery van.

Phil stood in the open doorway and asked, "Missy, what are you doing?"

"Damn, he's gone!" Missy answered.

Wondering what was going on, Phil asked, "Whose gone?"

"The delivery man. Phil, he was trying to kidnap me. He grabbed me and was going to shove me into the van, but I got to my pocketknife and stabbed him. He let go and I ran to your house."

The sudden appearance of a very frightened Missy was alarming enough, but what was he hearing? "Wait a minute. Someone tried to kidnap you? Just now, a delivery man?"

Still startled, Missy did her best to explain what happened, "Yes, he came to the house in a delivery van and handed me a box. I thought it must have been something Raine ordered. I was looking at the label and heading back to the house. That's when he came up from behind and grabbed me."

Phil joined Missy at the window, "You say he's gone? Where's Raine?"

"Raine went to the store. I was alone."

Acting as a deputy sheriff, Phil wanted to know, "Can you describe the van, I need to call it in."

Trying to regain her senses, Missy told him, "It was white, a panel type, with something delivery printed on the side. I didn't pay much attention to it. I know who he is."

This puzzled Phil. If she knew who the man was, why would she take the box or even approach him?

"What do you mean, you know who he is. Did you recognize him?"

Missy couldn't think of an explanation and just said, "No, I just know. There's Raine, I have to tell him what happened."

Missy ran out of Phil's house and up to Raine as he got out of his truck. The minute he saw her, he knew something was wrong. Why would she be running from Phil's house, and she looked terrified.

Missy yelled, "He was here Raine. He tried to kidnap me."

Shock and fear ran through Raine like a bolt. Somehow, he knew exactly who she was talking about. "Are you talking about the scammer guy?"

"Yes, who else could it be? A delivery van came and the guy handed me a box." Missy looked around and saw that the box was missing. "He took the box. The guy grabbed me and tried to put me in the van. I was able to get to my pocketknife and I stabbed him. Then I ran to Phil's. By the time I got there and looked out his window, the van drove away."

About that time Phil caught up with Missy and Raine, "I need the both of you to tell me what's going on. Missy says she knows this man who tried to kidnap her. How do you know him, and why would he want to kidnap you?"

Missy looked to Raine, and they both knew the truth would be difficult to tell, but they had to trust Phil. Raine was the first to talk, "Phil, we know who the guy is and why he wanted to kidnap Missy."

Phil was in full police mode, "Raine we need to call this in and put out a bulletin for that van."

"It's too late, I saw a delivery van on fire in a ditch off Cays on my way home." Raine had his suspicions, "My guess it's the van that came up here. There must have been more than one of them and someone picked this guy up. Phil, I hope you can trust me on this, it's really complicated."

Phil knew he needed answers before proceeding. He couldn't imagine how two people like Missy and Raine could be involved in a kidnapping and the torching of a delivery van.

"Okay, if the van is torched, we aren't getting much from it. How about the two of you tell me what is going on and why anyone would want to kidnap Missy. Kidnapping is a federal offense, and the FBI will want to be in on it. I have a feeling you guys would be opposed to that."

This time it was Missy who spoke up. It was her fault for getting involved with the scammer in the first place and she had to take responsibility.

"This spring I got involved with a guy trying to scam women online. He was using the identity of a soldier in the army, and it made me mad. I played an online game with him for months trying to find out who he was. The goal was to locate the scammer and put an end to the scams.

I also tried to find the soldier whose identity was being used by the scammer guy to let him know what was happening. The only upside is the guy was using the identity of Raine when he was a soldier in the army. Raine was eventually notified and that's how Raine and I met.

235

I ended the game with the scammer several months back, but a couple weeks ago he sent a text message to me. Since then, I canceled the phone number and no longer have the email address I used. Somehow he found me. I don't know what he wants or why he would try to kidnap me, but it has to be him."

Phil shook his head, "This is so strange in so many ways. I hardly know where to start. This guy could be working on his own or part of a scam organization. Do you have any idea where he's from?"

Missy relayed what she knew, "The only thing I ever found was that the phone number he used to text was issued from a company in Texas. The prefix of the text number is from the town Carrollton in Texas. He had a gmail account - StoddardRod@gmail.com. That's all I've ever been able to find out."

Phil shook his head, "Missy, I'm not going to tell you what a huge mistake this has been. The question is, what do you and Raine want to do about it?" Missy deferred to Raine who knew what he was going to do, "Phil, I know we've put you in a bad spot telling you this, but can you please keep it quiet until we figure out what to do."

Phil knew this should be reported. He would give them his advice, but ultimately Raine would make the decision.

"Raine, this guy could come back. I doubt he's seriously injured by Missy stabbing him with a pocketknife. He's probably mad as hell. There could still be something on the van that will lead to this guy. This is a small town, but even so, our law enforcement is good, and they may be able to find these guys.

This is not going to go well if you try to keep it quiet. I'll do what I can to help. I don't advise the two of you trying to find this guy on your own, but I suspect you want to. I can get the details of the forensics the sheriff will find in the van. I'm not sure there will be much of anything left."

Raine could see Missy was about to come apart at the seams. He wanted to take her in the house to relax.

"Thanks for anything you can do for us Phil. Please just give us some time to think about our options. My guess is those guys are good at staying out of sight and won't be easily found here in town. A search for them isn't likely to have any results.

Right now, I need a stiff drink and then we'll sit down and decide what to do. I'm sure those guys are laying low right now, especially the one Missy stabbed, so we have a little time."

Phil reluctantly walked back to his house and left Missy and Raine standing in their driveway.

Chapter 33

Missy and Raine stood in the driveway until Phil walked to his house. Both were stunned by the fact their wonderful world had suddenly been turned upside down.

Missy started to cry, "Raine what have I done to us? How could something like this happen? I've lived a very simple life. This is the stuff you see on TV, not happening to me, and now I've brought it to you as well. What am I going to do?"

Raine put his arms around Missy and held her tight. "Missy there is no 'I'. WE are going to do something about it. Let's go inside and we'll figure out what to do next."

Raine pulled out the tequila bottle and poured two shots. After he downed his, he poured one more for himself.

"Come on, let's sit on the couch and talk about what happened. I don't want you to blame yourself for what the scammer guy is doing. There is no way you could have predicted the guy you were playing that scam game with would go this far.

I don't know why he would come after you and attempt a kidnapping. He must think you know more about him than you do. This has to be a small operation here in the states, probably in Texas. What we have to do now is turn this around. We're not going to sit here and be victims waiting for his next move. We're going to Texas, find him, and stop the game."

Missy was still in shock from almost being kidnapped and now was amazed at what Raine was telling her. They had only been together for over a month, and he wanted to step up to protect her from a terrible mistake she made long before he met her. Was this something mysteriously passed down from his father or from his military training?

"I love you Raine and I can see you want to do something about what happened. These people are dangerous. I'm beginning to get the feeling you are not wanting to involve the police or the FBI. You want to go after these people yourself. Besides the fact that finding them may be impossible, if you do there's a possibility you could be injured or killed. I couldn't stand that."

"Trust me Missy, I can take care of myself and you." Raine gave her more explanation of why he was so confident. "We aren't dealing with a very bright person. Attempting to kidnap you in broad daylight in a neighborhood like this is really stupid. They will trip up and lead us to them. I have skills and allies that are equal to any law enforcement agency.

I know just where to begin. Missy, I need you to close your eyes and visualize the man. Start when he first got out of the van."

239

Missy closed her eyes and tried to see him, "He was short and husky. He had on a one-piece sort of work outfit that was navy blue, a baseball cap and sunglasses. I thought it strange he wasn't wearing a mask since he was a delivery man. He had a little more beard than you do, about a half inch long and black. I think his hair was black and short, but I couldn't see much of it because of the hat."

Raine had more questions, "What about his hands, did he have any type of gloves on?"

"No, but his hands were small."

"Did he say anything?"

"Not when he handed me the box, but he did when I stabbed him. He said, 'damn you'."

"How did his voice sound, any accent?"

Missy had to think for a minute since he only said the two words. "Now when I think about it, he sounded like a Mexican. I'm sorry Raine. I was looking at the box. I didn't think I ordered anything and if you did, I wondered who it was from. I was trying to look for a shipping label.

It was strange that he wanted to hand me the box. I should have been more careful. He grabbed me so quickly, there wasn't time to get anything off the box. Once I stabbed him, he let go, I just ran, and didn't look back."

Raine put his arms around Missy again and hugged her tight, "It's okay, you've given us something to go on and I have an idea where to start." Raine reached into his pocket, pulled out his phone and put it on speaker. "Floyd, I need your help."

There wasn't any hesitation, "Anything Bro, just name it. Hey, how's retirement?"

"There's a lot going on. I'll send you an email with the information I have. It will give you a head start while we make our way to Texas."

Now Floyd was intrigued, "Whose we?"

"The email will explain everything, got to go."

Things seemed to be moving at warp speed for Missy. She was pleased Raine wanted to help her, but he seemed to be going into superhero mode. Now they were going to Texas and who was Floyd?

Missy was at a loss and needed some answers, "Raine, what are you planning to do, who is Floyd, and why are we going to Texas?"

"All of the information you have about the text and email communication seems to be connected to Texas. You think the man who grabbed you sounded Mexican. That's where we're going to start.

Floyd worked with us on technical support in Kandahar. He's a genius with computers and a very skilled hacker. Floyd has just the right arsenal of skills to bring the scammer down. He lives in Dallas and if anyone can find the scammer he can."

It was now clear to Missy, Raine wasn't going to notify the authorities about the kidnapping attempt. He was going after the scammer himself with the help of the Floyd guy. The question now was could she stop him.

"What you're planning isn't only dangerous, but possibly illegal if you're talking about hacking. Don't you think it would be better to let the police handle this? I love you for wanting to protect me and stop the scammer but..."

Raine knew what he had to do and just how to go about it. "The FBI and Police get hundreds of scam reports each day. By the time they would get around to us, I hate to think what might happen. I'm not taking any chances. I'll email Floyd and then we're leaving. Can you get someone to take care of Puffy and the goats?"

"I'll call Sally. I'm sure she can take Puffy, and the goats can move in with the neighbor's goats. Are you sure this is the right thing to do?"

Raine's mind was moving so fast he wasn't taking in the effect it was having on Missy.

"We're not waiting for their next move. If you have an enemy, you locate, and take him out. We can't move on with our lives until this is resolved. I won't let anything or anyone ever harm you."

Missy gave one more try to discourage Raine from what appeared to be a military tactical maneuver.

"Raine, please rethink what you're planning. It sounds too dangerous."

There wasn't anything Raine wouldn't do to protect Missy, "You have to trust me, with Floyd's help, we will end the game."

While Raine emailed Floyd, Missy secured two airline tickets to Dallas. Calling Dotty and making up a lie she would believe about a vacation she and Raine were taking was a challenge. Dotty always asked way too many questions. There was no way she could leave town and not tell Dotty. She had to know Missy's every move. Missy hoped a vacation trip to Texas would sound logical since they had been to Connecticut to meet Raine's dad.

Fortunately, Dotty was busy getting ready for a trip to the grocer and was satisfied with the vacation story. She made the same flimsy excuse of a vacation when asking Sally to take Puffy for two weeks hoping that would be long enough. The neighbors and she had traded goat sitting before, so that wasn't a problem. They packed bags, got into Missy's car and headed for the airport. Everything was happening so fast Missy's head was spinning.

Chapter 34

When they walked out of the terminal from baggage claim Raine headed for a large black SUV with a very large scary looking man standing beside it. Missy had pictured Floyd Dunmore as a short, skinny man with a pot belly, a thin receding hairline, and thick glasses. He should be the typical computer nerd type, but this man was the opposite.

Floyd was well over six foot, built like Hulk Hogan, with a full beard, and a bald head. Raine, who is almost six foot and nicely built, walked up to him, gave him a hug, and was dwarfed by the man.

Raine made the introductions and Floyd winked at Raine with a look that said, 'way to go man'. They filed into Floyd's Escalade and headed to his home. The house was another surprise for Missy. It was an enormous, very modern, and a mostly glass house. Floyd had evidently done very well after his military retirement. With a few formalities out of the way, they settled in for the night, and would get started in the morning.

Since he was in Floyd's territory, Raine was willing to let him take the lead and asked, "Where are we going to start?"

Floyd gave them the information he had gathered, "With what we know. The text phone numbers came from the company Broadband in Carrollton, so we're going to pay them a visit and a listen. We'll set up shop in town. I made reservations at a motel we can use for our op.

Raine and Floyd began loading a vast assortment of boxes and cases into the back of Floyd's car. Missy was afraid to think what was inside the items loaded. Raine said Floyd was a tech wizard but hadn't mentioned Floyd's other skills or activities after his retirement.

Floyd seemed to revel in finding the scammers. As scary as he looked, his enthusiasm for this endeavor was almost as frightening. Was he going to put her and Raine in danger? At this point it was clear she was merely going along for the ride with these two ex-military men who were back in action and at war with the scammers.

During the drive to Carrollton both Raine and Floyd were fairly quiet. Country music was playing on the radio. Missy sat in the back seat trying to decipher what the two men were saying. It appeared to be some sort of code the military used. She picked up one phrase that worried her -It won't take us long to engage the enemy.

After checking into the motel, Floyd located the office of Broadband, parked on a side street, and walked into the building. They were in a run-down part of town and the 'office' was a seedy little hole in a block of closed up vacant storefronts. Missy was amazed at how quickly the 'operation' as Floyd called it had begun.

From the parking spot Missy and Raine could see through a window on the front of the office. A small young Mexican girl sat at a single desk near the door. There was a closed door behind her and it didn't look like there was anything else in the room. From the listening device worn by Floyd, they heard him walk to the desk and say, "Hola, I want two dozen text phone lines."

The girl didn't reply immediately, and Floyd wasn't sure she spoke English, but if she didn't he could repeat it in Spanish.

The appearance of Floyd must have shocked the girl and she meekly replied, "I'm sorry, for an order that large, you'll have to talk to Mr. Bramwell. He's not in right now."

Floyd didn't really care. Talking to the owner wasn't of any interest to him. All he wanted to do was stick the bug under her desk.

"Thanks, I'll check back later. Just tell him he has a customer wanting the text lines." Floyd walked out of the office with a grin on his face and a revitalized step. He was having fun.

When he returned to the car Missy asked, "What now?"

"We wait and listen. This is the boring part. My guess is that Mr. Bramwell she mentioned is going to get a call right about now from a very startled girl."

Sure enough, the bug worked, and they heard the girl make a call about a man wanting text phone lines. It didn't take long before Mr. Bramwell arrived and grilled the poor girl.

He demanded, "Who was this man? Didn't you get a name? What did he look like?"

Juanita wasn't sure who to be more afraid of, Mr. Bramwell or the man who just left her desk.

"He just walked in off the street. He was white and big, had a beard, and was bald. A mean type."

Bramwell pulled out his phone and placed a call. "Did you send someone in that I don't know for more text phone lines? Well, there was a guy in here today and he wanted about two dozen text lines. Is there a new player in town? Who the hell is this guy? Things are heating up. It doesn't help with the screw up your brother made in Washington. He's a loose cannon who went crazy for a mark that was never going to pan out. He might have blown everything up with that stupid kidnapping attempt. You should have kept better track of him.

This is on you, and I'll have some work for you to do. We need to do some house cleaning and move on with an expansion. I'll meet you later tonight. Call me, I'm not sure where I'll be. I have some business to take care of in Dallas this afternoon."

Raine looked to Floyd, "Well, that answers the question about who tried to kidnap Missy. That doesn't sound good. We're going to have to move fast. We need to know where Bramwell is going and what his new plan is. You made the first move and now it's my turn. Do you have a tracker handy?" Floyd handed Raine one of the boxes from the back of the Escalade.

"I'll be right back." Raine got out of the car and carefully walked up to the only car parked behind the office and stuck the tracker under the bumper. It had to be Bramwell's car, the office girl surely didn't drive a BMW.

Missy and Floyd kept an eye on Bramwell to be sure he remained in the office. After Raine returned from his task, Floyd slowly drove the Escalade away from the office ensuring Bramwell wouldn't see it.

Chapter 35

With their work done for the moment, except watching the tracker, and listening to the bug, they returned to the motel. The only voice on the bug was the girl who must have been talking to friends or relatives. She only spoke in Spanish, but Floyd and Raine were fluent and laughed at most of what she said.

The signal from the tracker was far more interesting. Bramwell drove to an address in one of the most affluent parts of Dallas. Floyd looked up the owner and found Carlos Juan Luis Alvares. When he checked several illegally accessed websites, it appeared there wasn't any record of a Carlos Juan Luis Alvares. He was a ghost.

Floyd spoke with a puzzled voice, "I can't imagine what a low life scumbag like Bramwell would be doing with a ghost who lives in a mansion like this. We'll put this on the back burner for now and maybe use it to save our skins later."

Missy again wondered why they would need their skins saved, but with the tactics Floyd was exhibiting, maybe they would. Raine said Floyd had an arsenal of skills and Missy was starting to see they were likely extensive and from the looks of him dangerous.

Sitting around a motel room wasn't going well for Floyd. He decided they could do some reconnaissance while Bramwell was in Dallas and the office was empty. After dark they parked on the side street again, picked the lock on the back door (easy for Floyd) of the office that was behind the door in the receptionist area.

They started a search of Bramwell's desk and files. Floyd found a folder with several sheets of typed paper. There were various short paragraphs that had the same sort of text and email messages that were sent to Missy. He pulled out his phone for shots of the pages.

Missy found a folder that contained photos of various military personnel. She thumbed through them until she suddenly stopped and held one up.

"Look at this. It's the photo the scammer sent to me of Raine in his fatigues standing in an airfield." Floyd snapped several shots of the photos in the file and especially the one of Raine. There were also some shots of ledger sheets that Floyd located. They carefully put everything back the way they found it and prepared to leave.

Raine opened the back door and was smashed in the forehead with a maglite used by someone coming into the office. He fell back against Missy who tumbled to the floor with Floyd. Raine lay on the floor unconscious with blood dripping from the cut on his head. Floyd quickly got to his feet, jumped over Missy and Raine and ran out the door.

There wasn't a light on the back of the building which probably necessitated the man using a flashlight. In the dark, Floyd saw a car driving away. Unfortunately, the man had enough time to get in his car and was racing down the alley. Floyd tried to get a photo of the license plate, but it was faint without any lights. When he returned to the office Missy was kneeling beside Raine crying.

Confidently Floyd told her, "Missy, don't cry. He has a hard head. He will wake up in a minute and be just fine."

Missy wasn't convinced, "Floyd, he's had a serious head injury before."

Thankfully, Raine woke up and assured Missy he was alright other than a headache and some bleeding. Floyd, in one clean jerk, ripped the sleeve off his shirt, tied a knot in the middle and wrapped it around Raine's head. They returned to the motel and Floyd properly dressed Raine's wound from the first aid kit in the back of the Escalade.

Finding the folders with the text and email paragraphs, military photos, and the ledgers was a pleasant surprise. The one thing they hadn't counted on was the man who came to the office and attacked Raine.

The tracker clearly showed Bramwell was still in Dallas, so who came to the office? He must have had a key because Floyd had locked the door after they broke in. They needed to be very careful from now on. The scammers had to know someone was on to them.

The question for the scammer guys was who broke into the office. It could be the feds, or they might suspect one of their rivals since a strange man, Floyd, had come to request text phone lines. Regardless, the scammers had once again proven to be dangerous.

Floyd kept a vigil on Raine for the next several hours to ensure he didn't have a concussion before letting him sleep. Floyd seemed to have a vast array of skills alright, and even some medical training. It was well after midnight before Floyd gave up, and Missy and Raine crawled into bed.

There wasn't going to be any love making. Raine had a splitting headache and Missy was mentally exhausted. Her sleep was fitful as she dreamed seeing Lyle standing in his doorway looking at a policeman who had a sober look on his face saying, "Mr. Stoddard, your son was involved in an altercation with a suspect".

Lyle yelled, "Altercation, suspect, what the hell are you talking about?"

The policeman continued, "Mr. Stoddard, I'm very sorry to inform you your son Raine has."

Missy woke up, eyes wide open and a scream wanting to escape that was silent. She looked over at Raine who was lying on his back with his head turned slightly toward her. She watched his chest slowly rise and fall with his quiet breathing. A tear ran down her cheek as she rolled over, laid her head on his shoulder and draped her arm across his chest. She would hold him tight until morning and forever.

Chapter 36

Raine woke up to a text message on his phone. "Stay put, get some rest, will call later with info."

He went to the door and saw the Escalade was gone, "Floyd left in his car sometime last night or early this morning."

Missy picked up the phone and read the text, "Where do you think he went and when?"

"With Floyd who knows. He's capable of some things you don't want to know about. We don't have much choice but to sit here and wait. Right now, it hurts my head to think. I need coffee and Advil."

Missy knew what he really needed, "Not without something in your stomach. Let's get dressed and find a place for breakfast."

After a breakfast Raine barely touched, they returned to the motel and waited for Floyd to call. When he finally got the call, Raine was livid. He put the phone on speaker.

"Where the hell have you been? I swear Floyd, if you've gone off the rails, I'm going to be really pissed."

In contrast to Raine's irate voice, Floyd seemed quite calm. "Settle down Raine, nobody's dead yet. Shortly after I got back to my room last night, the tracker on Bramwell's car died. Somewhere along the line he must have been rear ended or hit a huge pothole, and that's how the tracker fell off. The only move I had was the bug I stuck under Bramwell's desk when we broke in.

Whoever confronted us at the office last night called and told him about our break in. He was in his office before dawn to check it out. The bug picked up a call he made to the guy from last night. I could only get his side of the conversation.

He told the guy nothing was disturbed or missing, and he found Raine's blood on the floor. Bramwell said he would take care of Juanita. I assume that's his clerk I spoke to yesterday. He asked the guy if one of the men from the break in was a big guy with a beard and bald head.

He wanted to know what type of car was parked at the office last night. We need to get a less conspicuous car. Go to a used car lot and pick one up.

Bramwell said he was leaving and would meet whoever he was talking to, that's why I left the motel and am staking out his office. I have no idea how long he will stay in the office, so I can't chance putting another tracker on his car. He has a good description of me and if he spots me, he will go underground for sure. I'm going to try to tail him if he leaves. We'll get together later. I'll stay in touch."

254

With that the line went dead. Missy asked, "Does that man ever sleep?"

"Only when he has to. There isn't much for us to do but go car shopping."

Once again Missy was getting concerned about where this endeavor was headed. Raine had already been injured. Now Floyd was tailing a dangerous criminal and could be capable of who knows what.

Missy's next question was about something Floyd said, "What do you think Bramwell meant by taking care of Juanita?"

"That worries me almost as much as what Floyd might do. Don't worry, he's smart and careful. He will make sure nothing like what happened last night will occur again. We were caught up in the excitement of finding evidence. We're going to be safe and put an end to the scammers."

Regardless of what Raine told her, Missy still had her reservations about finding the scammer and putting an end to their operation.

Raine and Missy walked to a used car lot to buy a plain car. Missy looked around and asked, "What kind of car are we looking for?"

"Something cheap since we'll end up dumping it. The car has to be plain, fast, have room for our gear, and big enough to fit Floyd. There's a beige Honda CRV with tinted windows all around. Two grand's the sticker price, I have that much with me, let's take it."

The lot owner was suspicious about Raine paying cash that quickly for the car, but a sale is a sale and they drove away. There wasn't anywhere else to go, so they returned to the motel and waited for Floyd to either return or call. The hours dragged on waiting in the motel room. Both Raine and Missy finally fell asleep.

They woke shortly after dark with Floyd knocking on their door.

"I followed Bramwell to his house where he spent most of the day. You wouldn't believe where this guy lives. He has a huge house behind a gate and an extensive security system. He has to be into a lot more than just scams.

There wasn't anything to do but sit and wait until he finally drove off. He was headed into an industrial area with too many side streets. I couldn't risk staying close enough and having him spot the Escalade. I lost Bramwell's BMW on the dark roads without streetlights. Hopefully we can pick up something useful on the bugs tomorrow. I'm turning in right after I get something to eat. Come with me and we'll find a diner."

They walked to the same restaurant Raine and Missy went to for breakfast. Floyd approved of the car Raine bought and they planned to move most of the equipment in the morning.

Chapter 37

T he next morning Floyd, Raine and Missy sat together listening for the bug in Bramwell's office. What they heard was not good.

Bramwell might have been talking to the same man from the night before.

"You guys good with what we talked about last night? I don't care. You've screwed this up and now you're going to fix it. Things are going south and I'm not going to sit around and wait for the feds or whoever those guys were who broke in here.

We're moving up with Alvares. My meeting with him went just the way I wanted. When Juanita comes in I'll make something up to get her in the car. She'll make a one-way trip. You know what your job will be. Take care of it."

It was obvious Bramwell talked to someone from his house yesterday while Floyd was on stake-out waiting for him to leave, or where he went when Floyd tailed him.

The main concern for Raine and Floyd this morning was the threat to Juanita. The time was 7:25 and it was not likely Juanita would arrive for work before eight.

Floyd suggested their next move, "We have to get to Juanita before she walks into Bramwell's office. I know of a safe house near Dallas where we can take her. She'll be scared, but alive. Missy, hopefully you can make her feel less threatened.

Let's move now. Someone must drop her off since we didn't see a car parked near the office and there surely isn't a bus line nearby that area. Raine, I want you to make a call to Bramwell so he will be in his office and not see us approaching."

Floyd parked the Honda across the street and the three occupants slid down so not to be seen. The plan went great except for Juanita. Floyd jumped out of the car just after Juanita's ride pulled away. He grabbed her and she fought hard. He had to nearly choke her out to keep her quiet and maintain a secure hold on her.

Once in the car Missy did her best to console Juanita and convince her she was safe. Step one was completed with Juanita being taken to the Dallas safe house, but what was Bramwell talking about with the other man and what would his job be?

They also didn't know where Bramwell went the night before after Floyd lost him or where the other man was. Another question that bothered them was how many men were involved. There had to be more than the one man who caught them at the office. One call Bramwell made mentioned a man's brother, so there had to be at least two working for him. He also mentioned 'you guys', whoever they were.

It was also becoming clear Bramwell was into more than scams. That would mean there could be several men performing different tasks. Bramwell would be even more suspicious when Juanita didn't show up for work. If his plan was going sideways, he might move up his house cleaning work. The term 'house cleaning' was very concerning.

By the time they returned from Dallas it was dark which was fine for their next step. They needed answers and nothing had been recorded on the bug. Their only other lead was the industrial area where Floyd followed Bramwell. They entered the industrial park and drove as far they could until they entered the area where Floyd lost Bramwell the night before.

There were five side streets, each ending in a cul-de-sac. Floyd drove into the first three and didn't see anything suspicious. The fourth one was the longest with a large warehouse at the end quite a distance from any other buildings. It looked like a suspicious building.

Before entering the cul-de-sac, Floyd parked where the Honda was out of sight. If this was the warehouse Bramwell drove to, Floyd needed to identify any possible threats. There was a large SUV parked alongside the warehouse.

They watched three men leave the building and quickly file into the car. The car drove out fast. Floyd yelled to Raine and Missy to duck down as to not be seen. Unfortunately, the car was out of range by the time Floyd sat up to catch the license plate.

The parking area in front of the warehouse was now empty. Floyd drove to the building. They walked to the door which was unlocked. Floyd stepped inside and quickly turned to Raine. "Take Missy back to the car and make sure she stays there."

After a few minutes Floyd returned to the car. The look on his face told Raine they were too late. Floyd almost whispered, "There are about a dozen girls in there. All of them are dead. Some are at their desks, and some are on the floor. They look like Mexicans, probably illegals."

Missy was too shocked to cry. "Is this what Bramwell was talking about when he asked the man if he knew what his job would be? Is this the house cleaning he was talking about? Why girls, were they working the scams?"

Floyd hated to admit Bramwell was one step ahead of him. He should have been able to do something to find the operation center before this tragic end. Floyd knew Missy needed an answer but wouldn't like it.

"It's common to use women. They're easier to control and have various uses. I suspect Bramwell is into scamming, money laundering and human trafficking. We've stumbled into something a lot bigger than we anticipated. The warehouse has been emptied of anything useful. I doubt even the feds will be able to get any helpful forensics from the site. The only thing left inside was the bodies. I still think he's a small-time hood, since he wants to join up with this Alvarez guy. My guess is when we get back to Bramwell's office it will be stripped too."

Missy was now more mad than scared. "We have to call the police now. We're in over our heads."

Raine was the next to speak up, "We'll call the authorities from a burner phone after we're long gone from this area. We can also mail the photos of ledgers, other papers, and military photos we took at Bramwell's office to them except for the photo of me."

Floyd had another idea, "Let's also include the address of the house where Bramwell met Alvares. If Bramwell and his buddies go there, the feds will pick them up and our job will be done. I don't think there is any reason for us to continue. Missy's right, this is too big for us, and we can't get in any deeper.

The authorities shouldn't be able to trace the events of the last couple days back to us. The fake ID's and precautions we've taken should keep us anonymous. I hate what has happened, but I think this is the end of any casualties for now. At least Juanita is safe. I'll contact some people who can help her get settled."

Chapter 38

They drove back to the motel and packed their bags. Raine and Missy got in the Honda and headed for the airport. Missy was so disturbed by her thoughts, she was afraid to talk.

Raine spoke as they drove, "I know this isn't the result you wanted, and things turned out bad. Hopefully, the authorities will catch Bramwell, but we will probably never know.

This is a lot for you to deal with. I'm sure everything Floyd did seemed like something you would read in a book or see on TV. We started a search for one man and came across something we were not prepared for. I wish we could have saved those girls. Are you going to be okay with what has happened?"

Missy was still in shock and having trouble wrapping her head around the disaster at the warehouse.

"As bad as I felt about being scammed, it's nothing compared to what happened here. In a way I think we're responsible for the death of those girls.

If we hadn't pursued the scammer they might be alive.

This entire venture doesn't seem real. How did we get to this point? A couple days ago we were normal people living a normal life. Will we ever be normal again?"

Raine was not going to let the death of those girls be a weight Missy would carry.

"Missy, don't go there. Those girls were dead long before we got to town. As soon as they were caught up in Bramwell's business their lives were over. It's an ugly truth. I think Bramwell was ready to end his business here from the day of the kidnap attempt on you.

We had to do something to protect you from another attack. We were just too late to prevent what happened here. Please don't blame yourself. These types of things go on all the time. Just be thankful we put a stop to his operation in Carrollton. I don't know if Bramwell and this Alvarez will be caught. I can only hope so.

I know the actions of Floyd and I were frightening for you. This is what we were trained to do and I'm sorry to say this was normal for us. We've also been trained to cope with the results of our actions. We'll talk about what happened when we get home. I'll do my best to help you get past this and return to a normal life as you call it."

Missy heard what Raine said but couldn't imagine how she would ever forget or forgive herself.

When Raine and Missy got to the airport, Floyd walked up to them with a huge smile on his face.

"Bramwell wasn't fast enough. The call we made allowed the Carrollton PD just the right amount of time to get to his office before he could shred everything in his files. When they put everything together Bramwell will be cooling his heels in lockup forever."

Raine looked to Missy, "Coming here may not have been a smart choice, but at least we'll be safe now and you did get some justice."

Missy wasn't completely satisfied, "What about the three men we saw leaving the warehouse. They must have killed the girls. They can't get away with that."

Floyd reassured Missy, "Bramwell will most likely flip on them to make a plea deal. They'll eventually end up behind bars. My guess is the feds will also look up Alvares. Look guys, this operation didn't go as planned, mostly because we didn't have a plan. We had to go on what we discovered at each turn. Even the best op doesn't always go the way you want it to. Regardless, the end result caught the scammer. Each op has to take into account collateral casualties."

For Missy the stress and strain of the past few days caught up with her. She stood up to Floyd and yelled at him, "How can you call those girls collateral casualties? We were not at war. This was not a military mission. I just wanted to catch the scammer." She stood crying and let Raine hold her as the people around them began to stare.

Floyd spoke up, "Missy, I'm so sorry that we were not able to save those girls and calling them collateral casualties. I guess I slipped into my former military occupation more than I realized. I have to take the blame for everything that happened.

I should have been ahead of Bramwell. It just didn't occur to me he would have that large of an operation in a small town like Carrollton.

Please forgive me and let me be your friend. You and Raine mean everything to me."

It took Missy a few minutes to calm down. She could see Floyd was sincere and gave him a hug.

"I'm sorry, we never would have accomplished ending the scam without you. Maybe what you did was over the top for me, but I have to thank you. The scam operation has stopped and that was our objective. We all ended up safe, except for Raine's cut on his head."

Floyd gave Missy a kiss on the cheek, "If it's alright with you guys I'd like to make a trip up your way for one of Missy's tours of the Pacific Northwest. I'm going to need a little R and R too. It's been a while since I was on duty.

I'll call in a few days after you get settled."

Floyd shook hands with Raine and walked away. Raine hugged Missy again and said, "We need to go home and put all this behind us."

There was one thing Missy was sure of, "I'll try to put this behind us, but I'll never be able to forget it."

Raine and Missy stood watching their friend disappear through the crowd.

Missy had mixed feelings about Floyd. He stepped up to help solve something he wasn't even a part of. He was a good friend to Raine, but also a bit scary.

Missy remarked, "I feel like we're standing here watching the lone ranger ride off into the sunset at the end of a TV show."

Raine laughed, "Funny thing you should say that. Floyd was a ranger in the special forces before he was injured and ended up in tech support. We met at the hospital in Germany.

You should have seen us competing for the nurses and besting each other in recovery. He has been one of my best friends ever since. He retired and started his own tech support company in Dallas. I have a feeling he expanded the company to include some of his special skills too."

Chapter 39

During the flight home from Texas Missy and Raine were quiet. The thoughts that were running through their heads couldn't be said in a crowded plane. They would have to wait until arriving home before starting to deal with the past few days. During the drive home from the airport their exchanges were confined to small talk.

Missy was trying to figure out how she would explain her 'vacation' to Dotty. There wasn't a poker face she had ever been able to hide from Dotty. The training and therapy Raine had received in the military would help him handle his emotions. He would be there to help Missy and she needed all the strength he could give her.

The minute Missy unlocked the door of the house she knew she couldn't put off calling Dotty. Stress built the more she thought about the call.

She asked Raine, "What am I going to say to Dotty? As soon as she hears my voice she'll know something is wrong. She was suspicious after the way I sounded when I was kidnapped. She didn't really buy our vacation story either. I hate lying to her. If she knew the truth, first she would be infuriated I didn't tell her what was happening. Then she would hover like a mother hen and stress out. All my friends are going to want the details of our vacation. What are we going to tell them?"

Raine was at a loss for an answer, "I don't like the idea of lying to people either. Everyone, with the exception of Dotty, will be satisfied with a simple explanation. We can tell them we went to Texas to visit with a friend of mine and take care of some business. We should leave out the full description of Floyd and his activities.

If he comes to visit we'll try to get him to dial it down a notch. I don't know how much you want to tell Dotty. Maybe you can just give her the results and avoid the details. She's the only person who knows about the scammer isn't she?"

Missy tried to put everything about the scam and Texas out of her mind. "Yeah, after what happened in Texas, I'll never be able to tell anyone about the scam. It's unbelievable how it evolved into such a horrible ending. I want to forget the scam ever existed."

Raine knew he had to talk to Phil. "I'm going over to Phil's. He will want to see we're okay. I think he will be alright with keeping what happened to himself. There isn't any point in going into all the details with him either. No one beside Phil and Dotty should ever know what we did in Texas. Call Dotty while I'm gone and tell her what you need to say."

There was no use in putting it off. Missy had to make the call. Dotty would have preferred Missy to come over, but Missy knew she would fall apart and have to spill everything if Dotty saw her face. Missy placed the call with as cheerful of a voice she could muster. "Hi Dotty."

Before Missy could continue, Dotty yelled, "Tell me everything about your trip, don't leave anything out, especially the stuff you don't want me to know."

Missy could only think - 'There's so much you don't want to know.'

Dotty rambled on, "I've been worried and suspicious ever since you left for Texas. You were so vague about why Raine wanted to go. I know you said he was from Texas, but I also remember the scammer phone was from Texas. What have the two of you been up to?"

Missy knew there was no use trying to spin a short version to Dotty. She could see through Missy like a glass window.

"Do you have something alcoholic and a chair handy? I can't give you every detail. You don't want to know everything. You'll just have to trust me on that."

Missy started talking as fast as she could hoping Dotty would not interrupt her. "I got a text message from the scammer a couple weeks ago. All he said was - Hi Julie. The day before we left for Texas someone tried to kidnap me in front of my house. He faked delivering a box, tried to shove me in the van, but I was able to stab him and got away. I knew he had to be the scammer. Raine and I went to Texas to find the scammer with help from Raine's military friend who had the extra skills we needed."

Missy was surprised she wasn't hearing any rebuttal from Dotty. She must have been so shocked she was speechless.

Missy continued the saga, "We found the mastermind of the operation which encompassed a lot more than scamming. With the help of Floyd, Raine's friend, we were able to gather enough evidence for the authorities to arrest the scammer."

Dotty finally spoke, "I don't want to say I told you so, but I will. I warned you this game you played with the scammer was dangerous. Of all the crazy things you've done, this takes the cake. How on earth did you and Raine think you could even find the scammer let alone get him arrested? And what do you mean by a lot more than scamming?

I can hear pain in your voice. It's probably best if I can't see you or both of us would start crying. You're right, I don't want to know everything. I'm very fond of Raine and if he and this Floyd guy did something that's causing you pain, I might not be able to forgive him."

Missy felt she had to defend Floyd, "We never would have been able to find and eliminate the scam operation without Floyd. He was our greatest asset. He used to be a ranger in special forces and had skills that proved to be very useful.

He and Raine did the best they could, and the scammer operation has stopped. That was our main goal. I'm okay and so is Raine. It was just a stressful situation that has left me exhausted. Anyway, it's over now and I promise we will try to live a normal, quiet life from now on."

Dotty laughed, "How am I going to spice up my life if you become normal and quiet? Do you know how bored I was during those few days you were gone?"

Now Missy had to laugh. The stress of telling Dotty about the events in Texas melted away.

"Dotty, maybe you should get a hobby or why don't you get a puppy. Speaking of dogs, I need to go pick up Puffy. We'll talk more later."

Missy took a deep breath. That went a lot better than she had imagined and was a lot shorter than she expected. Thank goodness she thought of picking up Puffy. She really needed a good hug with that dog.

Raine walked in the house just before Missy hung up with Dotty. "Sounds like everything went well with Dotty. Phil is on board with our plan to keep what happened in Texas quiet. I gave him a minimum of details which he appreciated. He thought it best if this episode went away and was never discussed again.

He casually inquired with the police about the van fire saying he drove by and was curious. There wasn't anything useful and the police dropped it. Phil hasn't said anything to the neighbors about the attempted kidnapping.

Evidently, nobody in the neighborhood noticed anything out of the ordinary. Everyone bought our story about going on vacation, so we can say we visited my friends and took care of some business."

Missy felt the hardest part of their return was behind them. They still had a lot of emotions to resolve in order to move forward with their lives.

"Raine, do you think we can live the normal, quiet life I told Dotty about after what happened?"

He responded with resolution, "We can live any life we choose. It's entirely up to us to make our life what we want it to be. As far as I'm concerned, we'll be just fine. We have to be up front with each other and never hold anything back. I can live with what happened in Texas. Some lives were lost, but we very likely saved a lot more.

I know it may sound strange, but we fought a war. There were casualties, but we won the battle, and the world is better off. That's all we can hope for. Now I've told you how I feel. I want you to tell me how you're feeling."

Missy had so many mixed emotions it was hard to put them in words.

"It's more difficult for me to put what happened in perspective. From the beginning I wanted to find the scammer. I felt so violated for myself and for you. I never thought it would come to that end, but it did. It's easy to look back and see where I went wrong, but that isn't how it works. I'm not sorry for continuing the game with the scammer. He brought me you and you're right; the world is better off without Bramwell and the horrible business he was in.

Maybe the universe set all this up. I don't know why one thing leads to another. We try to make smart choices, but the outcome isn't for us to know in the beginning. There's a saying about hindsight.

I'm going to try and look at the good aspects of what happened and try to forget the bad. As long as I have you standing by my side, I'll be okay."

Raine gave Missy a hug and kiss. "Let's go get Puffy and the goats. We need to get our family complete again."

Chapter 40

Raine was anxious to get back to formulating the plans for a new house. He and Missy started going over the features they wanted to include. Missy's house was very nice with an open floor plan they liked, but it was too small. Raine wanted a bigger garage and a shop. The planning would give them something to keep their minds from going over the events occurring in Texas.

They had been searching for a piece of land that would be large enough for Missy's animals and would have a view for their house. A Realtor Missy contacted before their trip to Texas, gave her a call. He told her about a developer ready to plot an acreage into lots just the size they wanted and in the area she had mentioned.

Missy and Raine met with the developer and were able to pick out a lot that looked perfect. They wouldn't be able to start any work for several months, but with winter coming that wasn't a problem. The winter months would give Raine plenty of time to design an awesome home for them.

Life was starting to feel normal and quiet for Missy and Raine until they got a call from Floyd. "Hey buddy, how's life treating you guys. That sweet little lady taking good care of you? I've been thinking about that trip I talked about, making it up to your neighborhood. Missy up to playing tour guide again?"

Raine owed a great debt to Floyd, and he was a very good friend, but he was also heavy duty. He would take complete control of their lives given the chance.

"Floyd, you getting bored already? I would think the little episode in Carrollton would last for quite a while. If you want to come up, make it soon. The fall weather won't last for long. I'm sure Missy will be happy to play tour guide for you. She took me to some great spots."

Floyd had already made arrangements for a flight to Seattle. "I'll be there the day after tomorrow. Text me your address, but don't tell Missy. I want to surprise her."

Raine could just imagine the surprise Floyd would be. He wasn't happy about keeping Floyd's arrival from Missy, but he owed it to him. If Missy thought the man was way over the top in Texas, she was in for more than just a surprise. Floyd would be in full fun mode and full of energy.

Missy was working at her computer when she heard the cowbell ring and went to the door. She was nearly knocked over with the hug given to her by Floyd. Being breathless from the hug was compounded by the surprise of seeing their huge friend filling the doorway.

"Floyd, what a pleasant surprise! I remember you saying you would like to come for a visit and here you are."

Floyd walked over to Raine and gave him a big hug too, "I miss you guys. How about a tour of this beautiful place you guys live in? I have a reservation at a motel, but this town seems deserted. I know it's a small town, but the streets looked empty. Must be the virus huh?"

Missy gave Raine the look that said, 'you could have warned me'.

"Sure Floyd, I'd be happy to play tour guide for you. Just give me some time to make the plans. A lot of the businesses are closed. That's why the streets are empty. The governor has a stay-at-home order going too. Let's sit out on the porch with some beers so we can catch up."

Floyd told them, "That sounds good to me, the service on the plane flight was nil."

Missy needed a beer to settle her nerves after that surprise, "I'll put together some snacks too. Most of the restaurants are closed except for take-out now. After you get settled at the motel, we can meet here for dinner. I'm sure Raine will be happy to grill some steaks tonight. We'll eat about seven and bring your appetite."

Right after Missy said that she remembered that Floyd could eat three people under the table. Raine would need to buy out the steak department at the store. She would add baked potatoes and a salad too.

The afternoon was like old times for Raine and Floyd. There were lots of stories for Missy to enjoy and thankfully no mention of the trip to Texas. Quite a few beers were enjoyed by all. Missy was realizing the bond the two men shared and how important their friendship was to Raine.

No more than a minute after Floyd left for his motel, Missy had something to say to Raine.

"Why didn't you tell me he was coming? I almost fainted when I opened the door. With his skull cap on I didn't recognize him at first."

Raine could only think how stupid he was after the kidnap attempt on Missy. Of course, she would freak out seeing a stranger at the door.

"Missy, I'm sorry, Floyd asked me to let him surprise you, but I didn't think it through. Of course, after what happened with the kidnapping you would be scared by him. I should have let you know or answered the door myself."

To get even with Raine she added, "While I get my nerves under control, you can go to the store and get everything we need for a dinner large enough for that man.

Oh my God, I almost forgot. Dotty is coming over for dinner tonight. That's okay, she wants to spice up her life. Floyd will do just the trick. I can't wait for the two of them to meet."

Raine wasn't so sure, "You really want to do that to Floyd?"

Missy laughed, "Yeah, Floyd deserves a little surprise too. Knowing Dotty, he may regret coming to visit. Dotty has a distinct type of man she prefers. Big and burly, just like Floyd. She will be drooling all evening. This should be very entertaining."

Raine wasn't catching on to what Missy said, "Missy, Floyd is in his fifties like us and isn't Dotty late seventies?"

Laughing, Missy let Raine in on what to expect, "You've heard the term 'cougar'. Well Dotty likes men, especially ones with lots of muscles. Floyd will do just fine. Dotty ordinarily never wears makeup, but she has each time you've been around. Wait till you see her tonight."

Dotty didn't disappoint. Not only did she have makeup on, but was adorned with some very nice jewelry and fashionable clothes. Even Raine took notice. Floyd was immediately aware he had been ambushed. The minute Dotty was introduced to Floyd she took his arm and wanted to know everything about his friendship with Raine and Missy.

"I want to know all about the adventure the three of you had in Texas! I can just imagine all the fun things you guys did while taking down a major criminal. What an exciting life you must live. Missy told me you were a Ranger. How fascinating. I want to hear all the amazing stories you have to tell.

You obviously stay in shape. What type of exercise routine does it take to keep those lovely muscles? Maybe you could give me some suggestions for my workout schedule."

Missy was now feeling regret for sticking Floyd with Dotty. She was going way beyond her most obnoxious continuous monologue. Poor Floyd was at a loss without a chance to answer any of her questions before the next one came. He had an expression on his face that said 'help'.

Missy had to come to his rescue, "Dotty, I really need to quickly ask your opinion on the last page of my novel. It's something you're really good at checking for me. It will only take a minute and Floyd and Raine need to get the grill going."

Floyd gave Missy a look that said, 'thank you'. Raine only laughed after he stepped outside. Dotty was a dear lady, but boy could she ever talk. If you ever wanted to know anything about someone or something, Dotty was your source. She was the queen of asking questions.

As they started the grill, Floyd had to ask, "Whose idea was it to invite both Dotty and I for dinner? I gather she's Missy's friend and the one you mentioned that knows about the scam and our activities in Texas. I'm sure she's very sweet and a good friend to Missy, but WOW can that woman talk. She doesn't hold anything back either. What else can I expect from her?"

Raine didn't know Dotty very well, but suspected Missy could handle her. "Hopefully, Missy will get her under control with a couple glasses of wine."

One nice thing about steaks is the necessity to chew, which kept Dotty from continuing to terrorize Floyd. Missy also kept the wine flowing which she knew dulled Dotty and made her sleepy. This slowed her down enough for Floyd to casually answer all her questions.

He did his best to downplay their involvement in criminal activities and the unusual skills he possessed. The evening ended with dessert and port on the patio under a full moon.

Chapter 41

Missy volunteered to drive Dotty home. The extra glasses of wine and port were beginning to show, and Dotty's driving was sketchy when sober. She also wanted Raine and Floyd to have some alone time together for male bonding and reminiscing.

Floyd took advantage of being alone to divulge his alternative motive for the visit with Missy and Raine.

"Raine, I want to run something by you. Winter is just around the corner, and I've been thinking of spending those months in Arizona. You know how bored I can get and the trouble that usually gets me into. I have a new hobby, rock climbing. It has everything, athletic ability, great conditioning, and there's that much needed adrenaline rush. What do you think about that?"

Raine knew Floyd was the type of man who needed challenges, "Yeah, I can see you scaling rock walls. Why Arizona?"

"There's this town, Sedona, beautiful red rock walls, and it's a quiet place where you can get some peace. After what happened in Texas, you guys need a place like that.

I rented a huge house that pretty much has two sections. You guys would have plenty of privacy. It's important to have a rock-climbing buddy for safety and I need you."

Surprised was an understatement with that invitation to a winter vacation, "Whoa Floyd, that's a lot to spring on me. Missy and I have just started getting settled again, we bought a piece of land and want to build a new home."

Floyd wasn't going to give up, "You can't build in winter. Wait till spring and you'll have good weather. This will be good for you, and I'm concerned for Missy. We know how to deal with what happened, but I'm not so sure about the effects that will pop up for Missy. I'm sure she's tough, but that was a lot to take in on top of a kidnapping attempt. Getting away with new distractions may be just what she needs. Didn't you say she has golf friends that go to Arizona for the winter?"

"Yeah, Brad and Sally go to Scottsdale. They'll leave next week. Going away for a while sounds good to me, but I have to consider Missy. She has the goats and her horse. There's also Puffy."

All the answers to any objections Raine and Missy would have were already rehearsed by Floyd.

"Raine, she left the goats and horse when you went to Texas, and the dog is more than welcome. Look, no pressure. Talk it over with Missy and let me know. For now, let's just enjoy whatever tour Missy has lined up. And, please, can we leave Dotty home? She's pretty heavy duty, a nice lady, but I don't think I can take much more."

Raine once again had to laugh. He wasn't overly fond of Dotty at times, but she was a dear lady who meant well and if Missy adored her, Dotty was fine with him.

"Floyd, who's calling who heavy duty," teased Raine. "I think it's funny you finally met your match."

Floyd felt insulted, but smiled, "I'll let that one slide only because I'm your guest."

Floyd said goodnight when Missy returned from delivering Dotty home. One look at Raine, and Missy could tell there was something on his mind.

"Did you guys have a good time chatting while I was gone?" Raine filled her in on the requests of Floyd, "He survived Dotty without any scars but did request she not attend his tour. I had the luxury of teasing him about who was the heaviest duty.

He had another request that surprised me. He has a new hobby, rock climbing. He's planning to spend the winter in Sedona, Arizona. Actually, he's already rented a house that he said is large enough for us too. He wants us to join him in Arizona this winter."

Missy knew her life would change now that it included Raine. For the past decade she had made all her decisions based on only what she wanted to do. Regardless, he was now a part of her life that she cherished. She had to accept some of the decisions Raine would make. Just like going to Texas and hunting down the scammer.

All this ran through her head as she decided what to say about going to Arizona. She could tell by Raine's expression he probably wanted to go.

"It's not simple for me to leave the house and my animals. I'm not worried about the house or the horse, and I suppose the goats can go to the neighbors, but I can't leave Puffy that long."

This was an easy resolution for Raine, "Missy, I would never ask you to leave Puffy, she's part of our family. Floyd said taking the dog would be fine with him. He wants me to be his climbing buddy and it sounds like fun. We could also play golf there since Brad and Sally would be close by."

Once again Raine had that little boy look on his face. Missy could see the excitement building. He had made an effort to get to know her friends and spent time with them. She needed to return the favor and get to know his friends. Floyd was Raine's best friend, and she knew he needed to have his friends around.

The more she thought about it, where they lived wasn't important. Living together was all she wanted and if he would be happy in Arizona, she would be too. She could tell life with Raine was going to be a major change for her. Missy took a minute to think about the adventures she wanted in her life.

The adventure with the scammer didn't work out the way she thought, but it did lead to Raine. Now she had a really great partner for adventures. Dotty had told her playing the game with the scammer was foolish, but to Missy it had become a smart choice. Dotty would also be very unhappy having to spend the winter without her best friend.

Missy had a big decision to make. Life had changed for her the day she opened her door to Raine and now she had to go where it took her.

She gave him her answer, "I can see you want to go. This house in Sedona better be huge because I'll need some space between Floyd and us. He's your best friend and I know how much that means, but he's a bit over the top for me.

Yes, I like the idea of going to Arizona for the winter. Just to let you know. I will not be joining the two of you climbing rocks. I'm not even sure I want to watch. Promise me you won't get into competing with him."

Raine beamed, "Thank you, I know this is a big adjustment for you, but it will be good for both of us. We need a diversion and Floyd will surely bring that. Besides, the weather will be better, and I still have to whip your butt at golf. Wait till you see Floyd on the golf course. It's a riot. Speaking of a riot, how about taking Floyd to the lake."

Missy made a call to her friends Carol and Chet to see if there was a day they could go to the cabin at the lake. A plan was made for the trip to the lake in the morning. Luckily the great fall weather was still hanging on. There was one hitch in the plan.

Fitting Floyd into a pair of Chet's or Raine's swim trunks wasn't going to happen. They would need to stop at the sporting goods store on the way. Missy had a fear Floyd would be way too comfortable in his birthday suit. It was too bad Dotty would be left at home. She would have been drooling over Floyd's bulging muscles clad only in swim trunks.

Raine was especially pleased to show off his shiny new truck for the drive to the lake. Raine's description of Floyd being a riot was an understatement. He was all over the water toys and challenged Raine continuously with swim races, paddling contests, and underwater diving.

The two of them were such a comical pair, Missy laughed all day. She was content to sit and watch with Puffy who wasn't interested in becoming a water dog. She would be much happier in the desert of Arizona.

Once again Missy enjoyed the conversation between Raine and Floyd. She was seeing a different side of Raine and how he interacted with a man. Except for the days on the golf course with Brad and at home with his dad, he had spent his time with her. Every day there was something new she learned about the man she loved.

This time it was Missy who fell asleep in the back seat of the truck on the way home. Puffy was more than pleased to accompany her for a nap. It had been a long day trying to get the boys out of the water, but worth every minute of the time spent at the lake.

After another day trip to some beaches, Floyd was ready to head for Arizona. The goodbyes would be short since they would be together soon. For Missy, saying goodbye to Dotty was difficult.

Dotty promised to bring over Clark to help her learn how to do video chats on the computer.

Missy and Raine closed up the house for the winter, made arrangements for the horse and goats, and loaded the truck. They decided on a five-day trip with short drive days and some sightseeing on the way. This was to be just the first of many adventures they were to have.

ADVENTURES TO BE CONTINUED

Be sure to read *Dangerous Choices, Foreign Choices, and Deceptive Choices* with more adventures for Missy, Raine, Floyd, and Puffy.

Made in the USA
Columbia, SC
23 July 2024

38607773R00163